To David,

A Secret Witch?

Kelly led the way out of the woods and past the cherry tree. She glanced at the nail on the tree trunk where she and Jennifer posted notes to each other. "Hey, when did you put that note there?" she asked Jennifer.

"I didn't." Jennifer tore the note from the nail and read:

> Midnight is the witching hour.
> Then you shall be in my power.

"I never wrote this," she said.

"Well, I never did," said Kelly. She and Jennifer turned and looked at Adelaide.

"Don't look at me. I didn't do it!"

"Well, who did?" asked Kelly.

Happy Reading!

Linda Gondosch

May 5 '92

The Witches
⟫ of ⟪
Hopper Street

Linda Gondosch

Illustrated by Helen Cogancherry

A MINSTREL® BOOK

PUBLISHED BY POCKET BOOKS

New York   London   Toronto   Sydney   Tokyo   Singapore

A Minstrel Book published by
POCKET BOOKS, a division of Simon & Schuster Inc.
1230 Avenue of the Americas, New York, NY 10020

Copyright © 1986 by Linda Gondosch
Illustrations copyright © 1986 by Helen Cogancherry
Cover artwork copyright © 1988 by Judith Sutton

Published by arrangement with Lodestar Books, E. P. Dutton
Library of Congress Catalog Card Number: 85-25401

ISBN: 0-671-72468-1

First Minstrel Books printing October 1988

10 9 8 7 6 5 4 3 2

A MINSTREL BOOK and colophon are registered trademarks
of Simon & Schuster Inc.

Printed in the U.S.A.

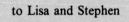

to Lisa and Stephen

Contents

Omen of Death

Kelly and Jennifer sat on the cold ground with their backs against the Geister family burial vault. Leaves of red and orange and brown swirled around their feet and over the nearby gravestones. From the hilltop mausoleum, they could look down past the small Baptist church and across Hopper Street to Rae Jean Greeley's house. Kelly stared at the old house as if she were hypnotized.

"The nerve of her!"

Jennifer jumped. "Don't scare me like that," she said and pulled her sweater around her shoulders. "The nerve of who?"

"You know who," said Kelly. "Rae Jean Greeley, that's who." She kicked a large sycamore leaf which had landed on her tennis shoe. "Good ol' Rae Jean. She goes and throws a big Halloween party and doesn't even invite us."

"We'll have our own party," said Jennifer.

"Oh, sure, some party! Who would come? There's no one left to invite. They're all going to Rae Jean's. She even invited Alex Bradford. Who wants a party if Alex can't come?"

"I knew it!" Jennifer laughed. "Kelly and Alex, Kelly and Alex," she sang.

"Oh, stop it. He's just the only decent boy in the whole sixth grade, that's all. And he gave me part of his salami sandwich yesterday. I love salami sandwiches."

"You love Alex, you mean. Kelly and Alex, Kelly and Alex!"

"Quiet, would you? You want the whole world to know? Anyway, the best way to a man's heart is through his stomach, my grandmother always says. And by the time Rae Jean hands out the apples and pumpkin pie and popcorn balls and chocolate chip cookies and candy kisses, Alex will be crazy about her."

"I'm getting hungry. Let's go to my house and see if there are any brownies left. This cemetery gives me the creeps." Jennifer shivered in the late afternoon breeze.

"Not yet. We haven't decided what we're going to be for Halloween. We've only got ten more days, you know."

"I think I'll be a cat. Remember that great cat costume I made last year?"

"Please. Don't mention cats. I hate cats."

"Oh, just because Rae Jean's cat won first prize at the pet show doesn't mean—"

"Yes, it does. I hate cats! She cheated putting that pink bow around Esmerelda's skinny neck. My parakeet would have won too if I'd put a pretty bow around his neck. I wish I'd thought of it." Kelly slid down the cold, granite mausoleum until she lay flat on the ground. She stared at the clouds overhead. "Say! I have a terrific idea!"

"What?"

"Let's be witches for Halloween!"

"Witches?"

"Witches! I saw *Macbeth* last month at Playhouse in the Park, and there were these three witches who danced around a black pot that bubbled and steamed. You should have seen it. It was scary!" Kelly sat up suddenly. "We could get witch costumes and a black pot, and tell fortunes on Halloween night and everything!"

"I don't know. I sort of wanted to be a cat."

"Come on. Witches are more fun. We could read all about potions and magic herbs and chants in that book I have, *Witchcraft and Magic*. And you know what else?"

"What?"

"We could become *real* witches!"

"Are you crazy? What are you talking about?"

"I'm talking about witchcraft, Jennifer, *real* witchcraft. My book says some people are born witches, but others have to learn the trade—sort of like learning how to be a librarian or a dentist."

"Well, I don't want to be a witch. Who wants to be an ugly, cackling, old witch?"

"Come on. Some witches are absolutely beautiful. You'd never know they're witches, they're so gorgeous. We could be one of those."

"I don't know." Jennifer touched her blond curls. "I suppose we could dig up witch costumes in my attic."

"Great! We could hold esbats—"

"Esbats?"

"Weekly witch meetings. I know all about these things. Of course, we'll just practice white magic," said Kelly.

"What's that?"

"That's where you do good things—like heal the sick,

3

help the crops to grow, stop hailstorms, things like that."

"You can't be serious."

"Of course I'm serious! I'm always serious." Kelly glanced again at the Greeleys' old Victorian house. "We might just do a little black magic, too. Just a little."

"What do you mean?"

"Oh, we just might learn how to cast a spell on Rae Jean's party. Ruin her stupid Halloween party or something like that."

"Just because we weren't invited?"

"Well, how do you like being the only ones in the sixth grade who weren't invited?"

"I don't," admitted Jennifer.

"It's embarrassing! I feel positively left out of everything. She's going to be sorry she didn't invite us. Real sorry."

"Adelaide Borseman wasn't invited either."

Kelly looked straight at Jennifer. "Adelaide? She's never invited to anything."

"Just because she looks like a horse with that long neck of hers and her big teeth. Gosh, Kelly, Adelaide can't help it if she's practically seven feet tall and the smartest girl at Riverview."

"Wait," said Kelly. "I'm thinking."

"Now what?"

"In *Macbeth*, there were three witches. Three! We'll get Adelaide, and we'll be the three witches of *Macbeth*. You, me, and Adelaide. We'll have our own secret coven in the woods behind the pool. Water's supposed to bring good luck." Kelly's head was whirling with ideas.

"And we'll practice white magic? Stop hailstorms and things like that?" asked Jennifer.

4

"That's right. We'll do only good things, things to help people. Except we might try casting a few little spells on Rae Jean—just enough to fix her for not inviting us to her dumb party."

"Shhh!"

"What?"

"Look!" Jennifer pointed toward Rae Jean's house. "Just look who's walking up Rae Jean's sidewalk."

"Adelaide!" Kelly and Jennifer sprang from their spot next to the Geister tomb and darted between the gravestones and past the church. They crossed the street and grabbed Adelaide's arm just as she started to climb the Greeleys' front steps.

"Adelaide, what are you doing here?" whispered Kelly.

Adelaide screamed. Jennifer clapped a hand over her mouth. "Mmghffmmbfg!"

"What?" asked Kelly and Jennifer together as they pulled Adelaide down the front sidewalk and across the street.

"You just about scared me to death!" gasped Adelaide. "Running around like a couple of wild banshees. What are you trying to do, give me a heart attack?"

"What are you doing here?" Kelly asked again.

"Rae Jean wants me to help her with math. She can't catch on to decimals."

"Oh, no, Adelaide," said Kelly. She pulled Adelaide past the church and into the cemetery. "You must never, *never* do that. Promise me."

"Why not?" Adelaide dropped her math book onto George Binkelman's grave and reached to pick it up. Her glasses slid to the end of her nose.

"Because Rae Jean is dangerous!" whispered Kelly.

5

"She is?"

"Like a vampire bat," added Jennifer, holding her hands in front of her like claws.

"And you know that Halloween party she's giving next week?"

"Yeah?"

"Well, it's going to be a very dangerous party. Extremely dangerous!"

"Good thing I'm not going," said Adelaide. She shrank back, tripped over Simon Pedecker's gravestone, and went sprawling into a pile of leaves.

"We're not either," said Kelly. "You're not going to believe this, Adelaide, but me and Jennifer, we're . . . WITCHES!"

"You are?" Adelaide squinted at Kelly through her glasses.

"And we've picked you to join our secret witch coven. We plan on being the three witches from *Macbeth* for Halloween, and we know how to cast spells and everything. We'll all three be witches. Just the three of us."

"You mean dress up like witches for Halloween?" Adelaide laughed. "For a minute there, I thought you meant you were *real* witches." Her loud, horsey laugh rang out across the silent cemetery.

"We *are* real witches."

Adelaide stopped laughing.

"I can prove it," said Kelly.

"How?"

Kelly pulled a pack of cards from her back pocket. She laid seven cards face up on Simon Pedecker's gravestone. Then she laid three cards below the seven cards. Finally six more cards were placed above.

"What are you doing?" asked Adelaide.

"Shhh! I have to concentrate." Kelly slowly turned another card over and gasped as she placed it in the lower left corner of the gravestone.

"What do you see?" asked Jennifer, leaning over her shoulder. No matter what Jennifer said, it always sounded dramatic. She was going to be a movie actress when she grew up.

Kelly touched four cards. "I see death!" she whispered.

"Oh, no!" said Jennifer.

"Are you sure?" asked Adelaide. She wrapped her long arms around her body and shivered.

Kelly looked up slowly. "Mark my words. There's going to be a mysterious death in the next twenty-four hours. It's in the cards."

"Kelly, look!" Jennifer suddenly pointed to Rae Jean's house. Rae Jean stood at the front window, looking out. Kelly, Jennifer, and Adelaide dropped to the ground and hid behind the gravestones.

"Are you with us?" Kelly asked Adelaide.

"I'm with you."

Esmerelda and the
Blue Sapphire Collar

"I'm going to be a clown for Halloween," announced Kelly's five-year-old sister, Samantha, the next day at dinner.

Kelly dug into her piece of apple pie. "Oh, Samantha, you're always a clown. You've been a clown ever since I can remember."

"I like being a clown."

"I'm going to be a tooth," said Kelly's younger brother, Ben. Dr. McCoy looked across the table at Ben. He was a dentist, and the word *tooth* caught his interest.

"A tooth?" Kelly laughed.

"Don't laugh," said Ben. "I'm going to be a back molar with a huge, ugly cavity. I'll get the cardboard box the microwave came in and paint it white. Then I'll smash a hole in the top and fill it with mud for a cavity. And I'll cut out two small cavities right in the front for my eyes."

"That's disgusting," said Kelly. She was thinking about her witch costume.

"It's better than a witch," said Ben. "More original."

"Move your elbow," said Kelly. "Dad, he's got his elbow on my plate!"

"I do not."

"You do, too."

"Kelly," Mrs. McCoy said, glancing out the window, "I think you have a visitor. Here comes Rae Jean."

Kelly sprang to the window and watched as Rae Jean walked through the backyard toward the patio. She carried her large black cat, Esmerelda, in her arms.

"Tell her I'm not home, Mom," said Kelly. "She's been showing off that cat of hers all over town ever since she won first prize at the pet show. I suppose she wants to show us Esmerelda's latest tricks."

"Esmerelda is a beautiful cat," said Kelly's mother.

"Well, I don't want to see it, or Rae Jean, either." Kelly flew through the kitchen and down the basement stairs. Dr. McCoy had just finished building her a bedroom in the basement.

"Kelly!" called her mother. "Is that any way to act? Rae Jean is a very nice girl."

The back doorbell rang. Ben and Samantha raced to open it.

"Is Kelly home?" asked Rae Jean.

"Sure," said Ben. "She just went down to her room. Come on in." Ben followed Rae Jean down the stairs and across the toy-strewn basement to the far corner where Kelly's bedroom was. He opened the door.

"Thanks a lot, Ben," said Kelly, glaring at him.

"Don't mention it."

"And next time, knock first, OK?"

Rae Jean held Esmerelda practically up to Kelly's nose. "Well, what do you think?" she asked.

"I think I wish you'd get your smelly cat out of my private room."

"Don't you see?" asked Rae Jean. "Look at her collar. Those are blue sapphires! My mother bought this collar in India."

Kelly examined the sparkling collar. "Are they real? Real sapphires?"

"Of course they're real. Do you think my mother would buy fake sapphires?"

Ben peered at the glittering collar and whistled. "Whoever heard of putting blue sapphires on a dumb old cat."

"Esmerelda is not dumb! She's probably a lot smarter than you are." Rae Jean put the black cat on the floor and patted her head. Esmerelda purred, flicked her tail left and right, and watched Creepy, Kelly's parakeet, as he hopped about in his cage on the dresser.

"Esmerelda is so smart, I thought I'd take her over to the Krebs' house tonight when I baby-sit. Their cat loves to play with her."

"You're baby-sitting for Marigold tonight?" asked Kelly. She had often baby-sat for five-year-old Marigold. Why had Mrs. Krebs asked Rae Jean instead of her?

"That's right. Mrs. Krebs called me and said Marigold had asked for me especially. I promised Marigold I'd bring my cat over to play with hers. I also promised to paint her fingernails red."

"That's bribery! No wonder she asked you."

"That's business," said Rae Jean. "You should have taken your bird over sometime. Or painted Marigold's fingernails red. Kids love that stuff."

"I never thought of it," said Kelly. She was sorry to lose her baby-sitting job. The extra money came in handy for birdseed and gravel paper.

"Of course, Creepy's so dumb, he would probably jump right into their cat's mouth when you weren't watching."

"Creepy is not dumb!" yelled Ben. He opened the birdcage and stuck his finger out to the little blue parakeet. Creepy nibbled his finger with his sharp beak.

"Close the door, Ben!" shouted Kelly. "Esmerelda will get him."

"Are you kidding? Esmerelda wouldn't hurt a flea," said Rae Jean. "She's not that kind of cat. I have her very well trained. When I say 'Come!' she comes, and when I say 'Jump!' she jumps. That's more than you can say for your birdbrain bird." Rae Jean laughed her shrill laugh and tossed her long black hair over her shoulders. "Esmerelda didn't win first prize at the pet show for nothing, you know."

"I could take Creepy straight out of this cage and he would stay right on my finger," said Kelly. She put her hand into Creepy's cage. Creepy hopped onto her finger. His tiny claws tickled.

"I like Ben. I like Ben," chatted the parakeet.

"See how smart he is?" said Ben.

"Hold your cat," ordered Kelly. Rae Jean grabbed Esmerelda as Kelly slowly brought Creepy out of the cage.

"Stay!" ordered Kelly.

"See that?" said Ben. "He doesn't even fly away. He's smart!"

But Ben spoke too soon. Creepy suddenly fluttered from Kelly's finger, bumped into the dresser mirror, and flew away across the room.

13

"Hold your cat!" screamed Kelly.

But Esmerelda twisted free from Rae Jean's grasp and leaped high into the air. Kelly screamed as the black cat's paws knocked Creepy to the floor and her jaws clamped around the squawking bird.

Ben closed his eyes tight. Rae Jean ran from the room, across the dark basement, and up the stairs.

3

The Full Moon
Ring Spell

The next afternoon, Kelly, Jennifer, and Adelaide did not say very much as they dug a hole in the corner of the backyard and lowered the shoe box into it. "I'm so sorry," said Kelly to Jennifer.

"That's all right." Jennifer put her arm around Kelly's shoulder. Only two months had passed since Jennifer had given Kelly the little blue parakeet.

"But I should have taken better care of him." Kelly rubbed her tear-streaked face with the back of her hand and looked down at the tiny grave.

"It wasn't your fault," said Adelaide.

"Yes, it was. I never should have let Creepy out of his cage. Why'd I do such a stupid thing?" She covered the shoe box with dirt and carefully smoothed the small mound with her hand. "There, Creepy. I'll never forget you. Never." She thought of how Ben had taught Creepy to talk, about how Creepy had fussed at the school pet show, about the day she had rescued him from the roof. Tears flooded her eyes.

"Come on, Kelly," said Jennifer. "We can go look at some more parakeets down at Murphy's. How about it?"

"No other parakeet could ever be like Creepy. I don't want any other parakeet." Kelly planted a cross made with sticks at the head of the grave.

"Rae Jean ought to keep her cat locked up," said Adelaide. "That Esmerelda is dangerous!"

"I wish she had never come over," said Kelly. "I'd still have Creepy if she had just stayed home yesterday."

"Hey, you were right!" Adelaide jumped to her feet.

"About what?"

"About a mysterious death coming in twenty-four hours. That's what you said. Remember? And it came true!" Adelaide stared at Kelly, fascinated. "You really know what you're talking about, don't you?"

"I told you I was a real witch." Kelly stood up and rubbed the dirt from her hands. "I think it's time for our first esbat."

"Esbat?" asked Adelaide.

"Our witch meeting. Let's meet tonight by the light of the moon, back by the sycamore tree."

"After dark?" asked Jennifer. "I can't come over here after dark."

"Just slip out. Nobody'll miss you. Climb out your bedroom window or something. The magic ring spell has to be done under a full moon, and tonight there's a full moon. I checked," explained Kelly. "And bring a broom and a ring. I'll bring the witch cauldron."

Later that evening, after the sun had gone down, Kelly carried the iron pot that her family used on camping trips to the small campfire area back in the woods behind her house. She set the pot on a stack of kindling wood and poured a jug of water into it. Then she struck a match and lit the sticks of wood under the pot.

"There!" she said as Jennifer and Adelaide joined her. "That's our cauldron of boiling water. Did you bring your brooms and rings like I said?"

"Brooms and rings," said Jennifer and Adelaide together.

"Are you sure you know what you're doing?" asked Jennifer.

"Of course I know. I've read all about this witchcraft stuff in *Witchcraft and Magic.* First we sign our names in blood in the Black Book." Kelly held up her old science notebook.

"That's not black," said Jennifer.

"It's brown. That's close enough," said Adelaide.

Kelly wrote *Kelly McCoy* on the first page and then pricked her thumb on a thorn of the wild rose that grew beside the sycamore tree. She pressed her thumb next to her name and held up the page with her name and the smudge of blood. "All right, who's next?"

"Me!" called Adelaide.

Soon *Adelaide Borseman* and *Jennifer Jackson* were written in ink under Kelly's name. Jennifer and Adelaide pricked their thumbs on the rosebush and pressed their thumbprints into the book.

"That wasn't so bad," said Adelaide.

"That's not all. Now," continued Kelly, turning to page

17

7 in *Witchcraft and Magic,* "it says, 'to be transformed into a witch, one must be sprinkled with the golden grains of the field.' "

"What golden grains?" asked Jennifer.

Kelly held up a box of Honey Crunch cereal. "Golden grains! See? It says right here, 'Ingredients: whole wheat kernels, malt flavoring, defatted wheat germ.' That's golden grains of the field." She crushed a handful of Honey Crunch cereal in her fist and sprinkled it on her head. "We are three witches of Hopper Street. Three secret words we must repeat. Turius, Murius, Zurius!"

"Turius, Murius, Zurius!" chanted Jennifer and Adelaide as Kelly sprinkled crushed Honey Crunch cereal on their heads.

"I just washed my hair," grumbled Jennifer.

"Do you want to be a real witch or don't you?"

"I do!"

"All right then. Now, hold up your brooms," said Kelly.

"Now what?" asked Jennifer.

"To give our brooms power of flight, we must grease them with the fat of a newborn piglet, belladonna, and soot."

"Oh, great. Where are we supposed to find a newborn piglet?" asked Jennifer.

"Quit worrying. I brought a piece of bacon." Kelly rubbed her broom handle with the strip of bacon and handed the bacon to Adelaide. "The belladonna was harder."

"What's belladonna?" asked Adelaide. Adelaide knew a lot of large words, but *belladonna* was not one of them.

"It's just some poisonous plant. I figure any old poisonous plant will do." Kelly pulled a large green and white dieffenbachia leaf from her bag. "My dad says if you eat this, your tongue will swell up like a balloon and you won't be able to talk. It *must* be poison!" She rubbed the leaf on her broom and handed the leaf to Adelaide.

"The soot part is easy." Kelly scooped up some cool ashes from the far edge of the campfire and rubbed them on her broomstick. Adelaide and Jennifer did the same.

"Wouldn't it be something if we could really fly?" said Jennifer.

"Keep your brooms in a cool, dark place for seven days. They have to age first," explained Kelly. Adelaide laughed her loud, horsey laugh, but stopped when she saw Kelly's serious face.

"Now, everybody hold your brooms in the air and repeat after me: Turius, Murius, Zurius!"

"Turius, Murius, Zurius!" The girls waved the brooms over their heads.

"Now for the full moon ring spell." Kelly glanced up at the huge orange moon just before it drifted behind a cloud. As the water in the cauldron began to bubble, a steamy mist rose into the darkness.

"I think I'd better go home," said Jennifer. "My mother thinks I'm in my room doing my homework."

"I climbed out my window like you said," said Adelaide. She was enjoying the excitement. "I practically killed myself when I fell into the juniper bush. See this scratch?"

"Quiet, witches!" ordered Kelly. "The full moon ring spell is very important. This is the first spell a witch casts for protection."

"From what?" said Jennifer.

"From anything dangerous. Come on, Jennifer. Quit being so difficult!"

"I was only asking."

"If you wear these rings, you will be forever protected from aliens from other worlds, monsters disguised in human form, ghosts, demons, vampires, werewolves, anything!" Kelly thrust her hand forward, fingers spread wide. On her ring finger was a gold ring with a red stone setting. "To work best, the ring should belong to a dead person." Her voice dropped to a hush. "This one does."

"Oooooh!"

"I bought it at the estate sale of Mr. Perkins, down on Rutledge Avenue. It was in a box of old junk."

"Well, we got ours from the machine at Benchley's Market this afternoon," said Jennifer. "Do you suppose they'll still work?"

"A ring's a ring." Kelly tossed her ring into the cauldron of bubbling water. Adelaide and Jennifer threw theirs in, too. "They have to boil for five minutes and then we light this purple candle. Witches always have purple candles."

"When do we start practicing white magic?" asked Jennifer. "You know, help bring good crops and good weather and things like that."

"We will. But first we have to put a little spell on Rae Jean's Halloween party. We'll fix her good for not inviting us. And maybe we could cast a spell on Esmerelda while we're at it."

"Esmerelda can't help being a cat," said Adelaide. "It's all Rae Jean's fault, I mean, about your . . . your poor little parakeet." She pushed her glasses up and smeared a streak of soot across her nose.

"Five minutes is up." With a long fork, Kelly scooped the rings from the pot and dropped them by the rosebush. She carefully lit the purple candle, then pulled a bottle of olive oil from her bag.

"What's that for?" asked Jennifer.

"Just watch." Kelly sprinkled olive oil in a nine-foot circle around the sycamore tree while she chanted, "No more fear, no more fright, three gold rings, shiny bright!"

The girls slipped their rings onto their fingers and stepped into the magic circle. Kicking their feet high in the air, they danced around and around the tree, holding hands, singing, "No more fear, no more fright, three gold rings, shiny bright!" Louder and louder they sang. Faster and faster they danced around the tree.

No more fear, no more fright,
Three gold rings, shiny bright!

"Kelly!" Mrs. McCoy called from the back door. "What on earth are you doing? Get inside this minute!"

Kelly, Jennifer, and Adelaide stopped abruptly. They doused the fire and quickly gathered up their brooms.

"Remember," whispered Kelly, "don't tell anyone. No one, I repeat, no one must ever know about our secret coven. Witches are *never* supposed to tell anyone they're witches. It's got to be a secret. Promise?"

"We promise!" whispered Adelaide and Jennifer.

Kelly picked up the purple candle and slowly led the way out of the woods, through the backyard, and past the cherry tree. She glanced at the nail on the tree trunk where she and Jennifer posted notes to each other. "Hey, I never saw that note. When did you put that there?" she asked Jennifer.

"I didn't." Jennifer tore the note from the nail and read:

> Midnight is the witching hour.
> Then you shall be in my power.

"I never wrote this," she said.

Kelly held the candle closer to the note and examined the blue stationery. A small yellow buttercup decorated the left corner of the paper. "Well, I never did," said Kelly. She and Jennifer turned and looked at Adelaide.

"Don't look at me. I didn't do it!"

"Well, who did?" asked Kelly.

The Poison Plague

The next day, Kelly, Jennifer, and Adelaide sat listening to Mrs. Ludlow explain how iodine solution makes the protoplasm and nucleus of a cell easier to see under a microscope. Jennifer yawned.

Kelly was busy cutting notebook paper into fourths and writing something on each piece. Jennifer watched as Kelly scribbled something on a piece of paper, folded it carefully into a little square, and tucked it into the cuff of her jeans. She stretched her leg slowly across the aisle toward Jennifer's desk. Jennifer smiled at Mrs. Ludlow, who smiled back as she continued to talk about how cell division could be observed under the microscope. Jennifer dropped her pencil, reached over to pick it up, and quickly snatched the note from the cuff of Kelly's jeans.

> Who exactly was invited to
> Rae Jean's dumb party?

Jennifer looked at Kelly and shrugged. Kelly continued scribbling all over pieces of notebook paper.

The lunch bell rang. Adelaide, Kelly, and Jennifer walked with the class to the cafeteria and sat down at their favorite table amid the sounds of shouting children, shuffling feet, scraping benches, clacking forks, clattering plates, and fussing teachers.

"Was the whole class invited except us?" whispered Kelly.

"Oh, not the whole class," answered Jennifer. "At least half the class, though. Alex and Matt are going. I know that."

"Amanda, Susan, and Patty are, too," added Adelaide.

"Who else?"

"I don't know."

"Well," said Kelly, "I've figured out a way to stop this party. When everyone reads the notes I wrote, nobody will show up."

"What did you write?" asked Jennifer.

"You'll see. The problem is, I've got to get all the notes on everyone's desks before lunch is over."

"I dare you to try to get past Mr. Johnson," said Jennifer.

Kelly looked at Mr. Johnson, the principal, who stood by the cafeteria door with his arms folded across his chest. Suddenly she picked up her glass of chocolate milk and slowly poured it on Adelaide's shoulder.

"Hey, stop it!" screamed Adelaide, shrinking back. "What do you—"

Kelly grabbed Jennifer and Adelaide and whispered into their ears. They immediately jumped from their bench and ran to Mr. Johnson.

24

"Oh, Mr. Johnson," cried Adelaide. "I just spilled chocolate milk all over my brand new blouse. My mother's going to have a conniption! Can I please go to the rest room? Please?"

"Go ahead." Mr. Johnson motioned Adelaide out the door. "Hold it!" he said to Jennifer as she tried to follow. "Where are you going?"

"I've got special stain remover. I always keep it in my desk. Please, Mr. Johnson, it's a matter of seconds with chocolate stains!"

"Hmmm, all right. Go on." Mr. Johnson waved Jennifer out the door. He put a firm grip on Kelly's shoulder as she tried to slip past him. "Where do you think you're going?"

Kelly looked up at him, closed her eyes, and put her hand in front of her mouth.

"I'm going to be sick. Any minute. I'm going to be very sick."

"What?"

"I hate the sight of chocolate gook on clothes, ever since my little sister . . . Oooohhh!"

"Hurry!" ordered Mr. Johnson.

The three girls flew to Room 19. Kelly handed out the notes she had written, and they slapped one on top of every desk except Rae Jean's. The bell rang.

"Just look at me," grumbled Adelaide. "I'm a total mess, thanks to you, Kelly McCoy! Did you have to pour chocolate milk all over me? Did you?"

"Adelaide, there are some things we have to do for the cause. You've got to do your part." Kelly pulled Adelaide out the door and down to the girls' rest room.

"You didn't have to dump chocolate milk all over me!"

"I couldn't think of anything else."

"Why couldn't you just say you had to go to the bathroom?" asked Adelaide as she scrubbed her blouse with a wet paper towel. She glanced up as Rae Jean and Susan opened the door and walked in.

"Are you kidding? That's too embarrassing," whispered Kelly.

"How do you think I feel? Now I'm going to smell yucky all day," said Adelaide a little too loudly.

Rae Jean laughed. "You always do." She and Susan pinched their noses and groaned.

Kelly and Adelaide made their way back to Room 19 and walked to their seats. Alex Bradford picked up his notebook and bounced it on Rae Jean's head. She squealed. "Stop it, Alex! I'm telling."

"Oh, boy, what a fake," said Kelly. "She loves it. How can Alex get near her?"

"Maybe he's blind," said Jennifer as she took her seat.

"Let's stop all this talking," said Mrs. Ludlow. "Settle down, class." Everybody grumbled. "Now we'll line up in rows to look in the microscope. Yes, Patty?"

"Somebody put a note on my desk. 'May the poison plague be upon all who go to Rae Jean's Halloween Party!'" she read.

"Hey, I got one, too," said Amanda. "It's printed real crazy. Look!"

"Me, too." Todd waved his note.

Soon the whole class hummed as notes were read, passed back and forth, and compared. "Who wrote these stupid notes?" demanded Rae Jean, twisting in her chair and glaring at everyone around her.

"What's the poison plague, anyway?" asked Susan.

27

"It sounds horrible!" cried Kelly. She waved her note in the air.

"I'm scared!" said Jennifer.

"That's enough!" Mrs. Ludlow smacked her desk with a ruler. "Whoever wrote those notes ought to be ashamed. Obviously there is a practical joker in this class." The class grew quiet. "There is no such thing as the . . . the . . ."

"The poison plague!" said Alex.

"Thank you. Now, may we return to our lesson without any further disruptions?" Mrs. Ludlow gave the class a look that made several students change their minds about saying anything more about the poison plague.

In a few minutes, Kelly and Adelaide stood bent over a single microscope. "Let me see. What do you see?" whispered Adelaide. Her head bumped Kelly's.

"I don't see a thing. No fingerprints. Nothing." Kelly moved the blue stationery around under the microscope. The yellow buttercup in the left corner grew large. "Whoever wrote this didn't leave a single clue."

"I bet it was Rae Jean," whispered Adelaide.

"No, I bet it was Ben."

"Your brother?"

"Right."

"Does he print like that?"

Kelly frowned and lifted her head. "Not really." She walked to her desk and stopped as Todd's leg stretched out across the aisle. A piece of paper was stuck inside his turned-up jeans. Kelly reached over and quickly took the paper, sat down, and read:

I'm not afraid of the poison plague.
Are you?

Kelly wrote a message and sent it back. It said:

> No, but I'm not crazy enough to
> go to Rae Jean's party.

On the school bus that day, everyone was talking about the poison plague. What was the poison plague? Who was going to the party? Who sent those notes?

Rae Jean stuck her foot out as Kelly walked down the aisle. Kelly tripped and dropped her books and papers all over the floor. "What's the matter, Kelly? Can't you walk?" Rae Jean laughed and tossed her long black hair over her shoulder with her hand.

"Yes, I can walk." Kelly snatched up her books and scrambled to her feet. She wouldn't go to a party of Rae Jean's even if she were invited.

Warlock War

That afternoon, the three witches of Hopper Street met again by the sycamore tree in the woods behind the McCoys' house. With a stick, Kelly stirred leaves in the boiling cauldron and peered into the water.

"The trouble is," said Adelaide, "we don't have a familiar. For a witch to have strong powers, she needs a good familiar."

"What are you talking about?" asked Jennifer.

Adelaide sat on a rock and read from *Spells and Hexes*, a book she had found that afternoon at the school library. " 'In order for a witch to have strong powers, she needs a good familiar.' "

"You're right! That's what's missing," said Kelly.

Jennifer looked puzzled. "I don't get it."

"A familiar is sort of like a pet," Kelly explained. "Witches keep pets like toads, bats, snakes, rats, and weird things like that."

"And these familiars have magical powers," continued

Adelaide. "They help witches perform witchcraft. Sometimes witches can even change themselves into animals. You might look at a cat and think it's a cat, but it's really a witch in disguise."

"Good!" said Jennifer. "Let's change ourselves into rats and creep into Rae Jean's house. That would scare her, wouldn't it?"

"I wonder if we could," said Adelaide.

"Right now, let's concentrate on getting a familiar," said Kelly. "We need some sort of animal. All real witches have one."

"Well, to tell you the truth, I don't want any bats or any snakes, either," said Jennifer. "I'd probably be allergic to them anyway. I'm allergic to everything."

"How about your basset hound?" Kelly asked Adelaide. "He's not much, but he's better than nothing."

"What do you mean, he's not much? Boris is slow, but he's extremely intelligent. He rolls over and everything. He'd be a perfect familiar!"

"We'll give him a try," said Kelly. She stirred the leaves around in the cauldron trying to see a pattern of some sort. The tall trees swayed in the wind. Leaves of red, yellow, gold, and brown fluttered to the ground. A few landed in the bubbling, hot water.

"Turius, Murius, Zurius!" cackled Kelly in her witch voice. "Spirits of the water, spirits of the sky, the poison plague is coming, that's no lie. Hee, hee, hee!"

Jennifer lay back in the pile of leaves they had raked together. "Some witches we are," she griped. "We don't know any decent chants, our broomsticks don't fly, nobody is afraid of our poison plague notes. Nothing is working."

31

"That's not true," argued Adelaide. "I wore my ring today, and I wasn't bitten by any dogs, or chased by Ernie Hinkle, or hit on the head by the volleyball in gym class, or anything. I tell you, I'm wearing this ring every day."

"You don't even know what other disasters you might have run into today if you hadn't worn your ring," said Kelly. "I always wear mine, even to bed." She gave Jennifer a scolding look.

"How often do you get bitten by a dog or chased by Ernie Hinkle?" questioned Jennifer.

"Well, all I know is, I usually get hit on the head by the volleyball in gym, and today I didn't." Adelaide held up her ring and smiled.

Jennifer turned over in the crunchy leaf pile and breathed in the warm, moldy smell. As her face brushed against something soft and furry, she screamed.

"Silence, witches!" scolded Kelly. But she turned quickly enough to see a small black-and-white animal about the size of a cat waddle out of the pile of leaves. "A skunk! Run!"

"Don't scare it," yelled Adelaide. She clambered off the rock, ran back for her book, and took off running on her long legs.

"Listen!" cried Kelly as she grabbed Adelaide's arm. They heard laughter coming from behind the bushes and found her brother, Ben, and his friend Buster rolling on the ground in fits of laughter.

"The witches are afraid of a poor little skunk!" howled Ben. He held his side, which was hurting from all his laughing.

"The skunk will get you if you don't watch out!" hollered Buster. He raced across the campfire clearing and

grabbed the skunk as it scurried through the leaves, looking for a place to hide.

"You're going to smell like the sewer plant any minute if you don't put that thing down," yelled Kelly. Jennifer stood at the far end of the yard with her hands over her nose.

"Look out, he's going to spray," cried Buster. He ran toward Kelly, holding the skunk in front of him. Kelly ran.

"Wait, witches! Come back," ordered Ben. "This skunk is harmless." He stroked the skunk on his head. "Buster's dad had him defumigated."

The girls walked back to the clearing. "Are you sure?" asked Kelly.

"Prove it," said Jennifer.

"You mean he took out his scent glands? He deodorized him?" Adelaide read a lot. She knew about things like that.

"That's what I said. Defumigated. This poor skunk couldn't stink anymore if he tried a hundred years," answered Ben. Buster's father was a veterinarian and brought home strange animals all the time.

"But what crazy person would want a skunk?" asked Jennifer.

"That's just it. Someone brought him in and then never came back to pick him up," explained Buster. "My dad says we can't keep him, though. I thought I'd give the little critter to Ben."

"I've already got Fritzi and Mitzi," said Ben. "I bet Skunkie would eat my frogs if he ever got the chance."

"I want him!" said Kelly. She reached for the skunk. "Does he bite?"

"Dad says he's safe. Here, you can have him." Buster handed the skunk to Kelly.

"Are you crazy?" asked Adelaide. "Only crazy people have skunks for pets."

"Aw, I think he's cute," said Kelly. She petted the skunk and was surprised at how silky his black-and-white fur felt.

"Yeah, and he'll make a terrific familiar!" Ben said with a laugh. "Every *witch* needs a good familiar."

Kelly's head jerked up. "This is our *secret* coven, Ben. You and Buster just forget everything you saw here today, OK?"

"Why should we?"

"We are very serious witches," Adelaide began.

"Wait, Adelaide!" Kelly turned to Ben and Buster. "Just how much did you see, you big snoops?"

"Enough to know that you are very serious witches," shouted Ben. He danced around the campfire. "Turius, Murius, Zurius!" Buster joined him and the two hopped around the cauldron, cackling with glee, like a pair of impish woodland elves.

Kelly slapped her forehead and dropped onto the rock. "We're ruined. Ruined! Ben always has to come snooping around, spoiling everything. I never have any privacy!" She groaned. The skunk looked up at her.

Ben stirred the pot of boiling leaves with the stick. "I see mysterious things brewing in the future," he said in a ghostly voice. "Yes, yes! Adelaide will become a famous chicken plucker and move to Timbuktu, Kelly will marry a big ugly gorilla and move to the zoo, Jennifer will—"

"Oh, shut up, Ben! Go soak your head, would you?" said Kelly.

Buster grabbed the stick from Ben, and they danced around the bubbling cauldron singing, "The poison plague is coming, and that's no lie. If you don't believe me, I'll spit in your eye. Ha ha ha!"

"Shows how much you know. The poison plague *is* coming!" said Kelly. "To anyone going to Rae Jean's party."

"What's the poison plague?" asked Ben.

"That's a secret. Only coven members know."

"Well, Buster and I want to be members, don't we, Buster?"

"Yeah! Do you serve refreshments?"

"Of course," said Jennifer. "We drink the blood of bats and eat dried rattlesnake skins and the flesh of wild pigs. Mmm, good!"

"I like our lizards' claws and the pickled intestinal worms!" said Kelly. "Delicious."

"No, no," added Adelaide. "Pulverized hummingbirds and monkey fat are my favorites. Just thinking about those hummingbirds makes my mouth water."

"Gee, that sounds great!" said Ben. "We want to join. Right, Buster?"

"Right! I'm getting hungry."

"Well, you can't!" said Kelly. "This is our own private club. We don't want you pestering us. Now get lost!"

"Make us!" said Buster.

"We want to join," insisted Ben.

"Do you really have a rattlesnake skin?" Buster asked, looking around.

"Get out of here!" cried Kelly.

"If you don't let us join, we're telling everybody in

school who wrote those notes. What do you think about that?" Ben threw the stick on the ground and turned to go.

"No, wait!" called Kelly. "You can't do that."

"Who's going to stop us?"

"Rae Jean will kill us!" said Jennifer in her most dramatic voice.

"They'll never stop laughing," said Adelaide.

"This should be good," said Buster. He followed Ben across the backyard. Wherever Ben went, Buster was usually not far behind.

"And wait 'til we tell everybody you're witches," added Ben, "real witches in disguise."

"Come back, Ben. Come back and we'll . . . we'll let you join our coven!"

Ben smiled at Buster. They ran back across the yard, jumped over the rock, and landed in the leaf pile. "You mean we can be witches?"

"You'll be warlocks," said Kelly. "That's what male witches are called. Real warlocks with real powers!" She spoke in a loud whisper. "But you have to keep it quiet. Understand? Quiet. Witchcraft is something that has to be kept a secret." She held her finger to her lips.

"I'm good at keeping secrets," said Buster.

"Warlock," said Ben. "That sounds scary. Maybe I'll be that instead of a tooth for Halloween."

"This is for real. Witches and warlocks meet in secret covens and plan their witchcraft. Right now, we're planning to put a hex on Rae Jean's Halloween party. After that, we'll work on bringing some good weather and making the crops grow."

"Crops don't grow in the winter, dummy," said Ben.

"I'll tell you what we need—a good snowstorm," suggested Buster. "Last year the sledding was rotten."

"OK, we'll join," said Ben. "But only if I get to be the chief warlock."

"You'll get your turn, Ben. First you have to be admitted by signing your name in blood in the Black Book." Kelly pulled out her science notebook.

"Hey, this is great! Blood and everything!" said Ben.

"Sign here, Ben McCoy." Ben took the pen and signed. Adelaide pulled him over to the rosebush and pricked his thumb on a thorn.

"Ouch!"

"Please, we must have silence," said Kelly in her most serious voice. She stirred the pot of bubbling leaves.

"Do we have to have Ben and Buster in our coven? They'll ruin everything," whispered Jennifer in her ear.

"Do we really have any choice?" whispered Kelly.

The Witch
Initiation Ceremony

"You know," said Adelaide, "this book says that to become an official witch, you must rub your body with parsley and belladonna, drink salted water, and eat the meat of a chicken's liver."

"Where does it say that?" asked Ben, astonished.

"Right here." Adelaide pointed to page 29 in *Spells and Hexes.*

"You said hummingbirds, not chicken liver! I hate chicken liver!"

"I'd rather eat chicken liver than a hummingbird any day," insisted Adelaide.

"I can't eat chicken liver. It gives me warts," argued Ben.

"Good! Witches are supposed to have warts," said Adelaide.

"Will we get warts on the ends of our noses?" asked Buster.

"Isn't that where witches always get them?" answered Adelaide.

"I don't want an ugly wart on my nose," said Jennifer. "I refuse to eat any chicken liver."

"She's only joking, Jen," said Kelly. "You're not going to get warts."

"Do we really have to do all those things?" asked Ben.

"This is for a witch initiation. That's what this book says, if you want to be an official witch," stated Adelaide. She wiped her glasses on her sleeve and set them back on her nose.

"Did you rub your bodies with parsley and all that other stuff?" asked Ben.

"No," answered Kelly.

"Then *you* have to, too."

"Oh, Adelaide! Did you have to read that?" asked Jennifer.

"It shouldn't be all that hard. Don't you have parsley in your kitchen?"

"I bet we do," said Kelly. "But where will we find chicken livers? All we've got in the freezer is some frozen baby beef liver. I saw some when I was hunting for the ice cream. Mom always hides the ice cream in the back of the freezer."

"Beef liver, chicken liver. Liver is liver," said Adelaide. She snapped the book shut. "My mom makes liver with onions and bacon all the time. I hate it, but if that's what it takes to become an official witch, then . . . I'll do it!"

"Liver? Yuck!" yelled Ben.

"All right," said Kelly. "If we're going to do this, we're going to do it right. Bring your book, Adelaide." They all followed Kelly out of the woods, through the backyard, and into the garage. Kelly dropped her skunk into a large box and carried him to the patio. "I'd better leave him outside for now," she said as she placed the box next to the picnic table. She led the way into the kitchen.

"OK, here's some parsley." Kelly pulled up her sleeves, shook parsley on her arm, and rubbed it from her hand to her elbow. Then she rubbed her other arm and passed the can of parsley to Jennifer. She pulled a large green-and-white leaf from the dieffenbachia plant in the family room and crumpled it in her hand.

"What's that for?"

"Didn't you say you have to rub your body with belladonna, the poisonous plant?"

"Yeah."

"This is all we've got. This thing is poisonous."

Kelly, Jennifer, Adelaide, Ben, and Buster stood around the kitchen table and rubbed their faces, necks, arms, and legs with parsley and crumpled dieffenbachia leaves. They could hear Mrs. McCoy in the basement running the sweeper.

"Go on. What's next?" asked Kelly.

"To become a witch, we must drink salted water," stated Adelaide, checking her book.

"How much?" asked Jennifer.

"One swallow should do it," said Adelaide.

"Heck, that's no worse than gargling," said Ben.

"Yeah, except this we have to swallow."

"I always swallow the gargle. I can't help it."

They shook salt into a glass of water, stirred it, then passed it around. Each one wiped the glass on a sleeve, turned it a little, and took a sip.

41

"Blaghg!" said Jennifer. She stuck out her tongue. "I think I'm going to be sick."

"Not yet. We still have to eat the baby beef liver," said Kelly. She opened the freezer and pulled out a package of baby beef liver. "Mom always has some of this. She loves it."

"She loves spinach, too, and Elvis Presley," said Ben.

"Adults are weird sometimes," said Adelaide.

Kelly dumped the frozen block of liver into the skillet and turned on the heat. They threw in butter, bacon, onions, and leftover spaghetti sauce to kill the taste. "We've got to hurry," said Kelly. Mom sounds like she's almost done downstairs. And Dad's due home any minute."

It wasn't too long before the five of them gathered around the kitchen table and speared small pieces of liver, dripping with spaghetti sauce and onions, onto their forks.

"Ugh!" Jennifer pinched her nose with one hand and held her fork with the other. "I think I'm allergic to liver. I just happened to remember." She put her fork down.

"You are not!" said Ben.

"Witches, warlocks, do not cheat. All this liver you must eat!" chanted Kelly.

"All of it?" asked Ben. He took a bite and began to chew. "Being an official warlock is rough!"

"Close your mouth when you chew, please, Ben," said Kelly.

Just then Samantha walked into the kitchen, dragging her torn old blanket behind her. "Something stinks," she said. "What are you eating?"

"Liver. It's delicious!" said Kelly.

"You can't have any," said Ben.

"Why can't I have any?" Samantha climbed onto a chair. "Who says I can't have any? I'm telling!"

"If you insist," said Kelly. She jumped up, grabbed another plate and fork, and gave Samantha a piece of her liver. "Taste this. You'll love it."

"Hmmm," said Samantha. "I like it!"

Mrs. McCoy came up the basement stairs and into the kitchen. "What in the world is going on here?" she asked as she looked at the six children seated around the kitchen table, each with a plateful of liver.

"We're having a liver party," said Ben.

"A liver party?"

"Gosh, Mom, didn't you ever have a liver party when you were a kid?"

"No, I never did."

"Well, you'll never know what you missed."

"We're putting iron and vitamins into our bodies," said Kelly.

"We're building up our red corpuscles," explained Adelaide. She loved using big words.

Samantha smiled. "I want more!"

"Here, you can have mine," said Ben.

"I think I'll go sweep out the garage," said Mrs. McCoy with a sigh.

"Don't you want any liver? It's really tasty."

"No thanks." Mrs. McCoy opened the back door and walked to the garage.

"What's wrong with your mom?" asked Jennifer.

"She looked confused," said Adelaide.

"She's always a little confused," said Kelly, "ever since she went back to work. I don't think she gets enough sleep."

"Maybe not enough liver," said Jennifer. "She can have mine."

"I'll take it," said Buster. "This isn't bad." They all looked at Buster as though he were crazy and then dumped all their liver onto his plate.

"Ben!" cried Mrs. McCoy, coming back into the kitchen. "What on earth did you do to my broom?" She held up the greasy, sooty broom. "This is a mess!"

"I didn't do anything."

Kelly jumped up from the table. "Don't touch it, Mom. It's aging!" she said too quickly.

"It's what?"

"It's a . . . an experiment I have to do for science class. What I did was—"

"Kelly," interrupted Mrs. McCoy, "just clean up this mess, would you, please?" She handed the broom to Kelly.

"I will, Mom. I promise." Mrs. McCoy returned to the garage. The children quickly washed all the dishes and then ran back to the woods. Samantha followed.

"You can't come with us," said Kelly.

"Why not?" asked Samantha.

"Here." Kelly reached into her pocket and gave Samantha a stick of gum. "Now go play with Marigold."

"OK." Samantha popped the gum into her mouth and ran off to look for Marigold.

Finally the witches gathered once more around the sycamore tree. With a stick, Kelly drew a nine-foot circle around the tree and ordered everyone to sit down inside the circle. "Now that we are all official witches"—Kelly glanced at Ben and Buster—"and warlocks, we will discuss our first order of witch business. It's about this note." She pulled the piece of blue stationery from her pocket and read: " 'Midnight is the witching hour. Then you shall be in my power.' Come on, Ben. Did you tack this note to the cherry tree?"

"Me? Uh . . . maybe and maybe not."

"I think he did," said Jennifer. "He looks guilty."

"OK, I did."

"You can't write that well, Ben. Look at these beautiful letters," said Adelaide.

"OK, I didn't."

"Did you or didn't you?" asked Kelly.

"I never wrote it. Honest."

"He looks guilty," said Jennifer.

"The question is," said Kelly with a worried look spreading across her face, "who did?"

They all looked at each other as they realized that not one of them had written the mysterious note. "Somebody is going to put us in their power. At midnight. Maybe tonight." said Jennifer.

"Who would want to do that?" asked Adelaide.

"The trouble is," said Kelly, "we don't have strong enough powers to do anything. Even our poison plague scare isn't working."

"Our rings are working," said Adelaide.

"It's not enough." Kelly flipped through the pages of *Witchcraft and Magic* and stopped on page 43. "It says right here: 'To gain magical energy and strengthen one's powers as a witch, one must bury a good luck charm by the light of the moon.' "

"Wow!" said Buster. "Are we going to do that?"

"We must strengthen our powers," stated Kelly. "That's our whole problem. We've got rings to protect us, but we don't have enough magical energy to carry out our witchcraft."

"Let me see the rings," said Ben. He and Buster studied the three rings which the girls held up.

"We'll get your rings later. Right now we need a good luck charm to bury. And we'll have to bury it tonight by the light of the moon."

"Right here where *X* marks the spot," said Buster. He scratched an *X* in the dirt beside the tree.

"Good thinking," said Ben. "Now, who has a good luck charm?"

"Just a minute. I need Cinnamon to help me think," said Kelly.

"Who's Cinnamon?"

"My familiar. You know, the skunk."

"What a stupid name," said Ben.

"Look, I figure if I feed him cinnamon and sugar and nutmeg and stuff like that every morning, he'll smell really good. You are what you eat, Grandma always says."

"Dumb," said Ben.

Kelly ran out of the woods and all the way to the patio, where she pulled Cinnamon from his cardboard box. She hurried back to the circle.

"Has anyone thought of a good luck charm we can bury tonight?" she asked on her return. "Come on, witches, think of something!"

"How about your white lucky stone?" Buster asked Ben. "That one you found last week in the cemetery?"

"I traded that to Alex for a Pete Rose baseball card."

"I wanted that card!" said Buster.

"Too late."

"Hey, Buster," called Kelly. "Do you still have your lucky rabbit's foot?"

Buster slapped his hand across his back pocket. "No!"

"Yes, you do. Come on, hand it over," said Kelly.

"No! I traded it. . . . I traded it for a . . . for a . . ."

"Buster! This is important. We need it," insisted Kelly.

"You're not burying my rabbit's foot." Buster reached into his back pocket and pulled out the rabbit's foot. "It'll get all dirty. This was expensive."

"Come on. We can always dig it up again tomorrow," said Kelly. "We really must strengthen our powers. Don't you want to be a strong warlock, able to bring on a good snowstorm, enough to get school canceled?"

"Hmmm. Oh, OK. Here." Buster tossed the rabbit's foot over to Kelly.

"Great. Now, everyone meet here tonight at midnight and we'll bury it."

" 'Midnight is the witching hour. Then you shall be in my power,' " chanted Jennifer.

"On second thought," said Kelly, "make it nine o'clock. We have to increase our powers *before* midnight."

At nine o'clock, the large orange moon was high in the October sky. Ben dug a small hole inside the nine-foot circle. Kelly sat, holding Cinnamon, and looked around at the dark, waving branches of the trees. She heard the hoot of a distant owl.

"I guess Jennifer and Adelaide couldn't slip out," she said.

"Maybe Adelaide fell into her juniper bush and got stuck," said Buster. He began to laugh.

"Shhh!" warned Kelly. "Just bury that thing and let's get out of here. 'To gain magical energy and strengthen one's powers as a witch, one must bury a good luck charm by the light of the moon.' This should help matters." Buster dropped his rabbit's foot into the hole and covered it up with dirt.

"Boo!" yelled Adelaide and Jennifer together. Kelly jerked around and dropped Cinnamon. Instead of running away, the skunk curled up in a circle by her feet.

"Scare us to death, why don't you?" scolded Kelly. But she was glad to see her friends. The five of them joined hands around the sycamore tree inside the magic, nine-foot circle.

"The rabbit is buried," stated Kelly solemnly.

"Rabbit's foot," corrected Buster. "And I get it back tomorrow."

"You will, don't worry. Now, our next business is to make a voodoo doll. We'll make a little doll out of Play Doh or something and make it look just like Rae Jean. To make it work, we have to stuff it full of Rae Jean's hair, fingernail clippings, and even pieces of her clothes.

"Why?" asked Adelaide.

"Because with a voodoo doll, a witch gains control over whoever the doll looks like. And if we stick pins into the doll's head, Rae Jean will get a terrific headache. Maybe then she'll have to call off her Halloween party. Serve her right for not inviting us."

"Yeah!" agreed Jennifer.

"Maybe she didn't invite you 'cause you never invited her to your birthday party last summer," said Ben. "Remember?"

49

"I hardly knew her then. They only moved here in June. Anyway, tomorrow we're going to spy on Rae Jean's garage sale and see what we can find."

"People don't sell hair and fingernails at garage sales," said Ben. He squeezed her hand hard.

"Ouch! I know that, Ben. We'll find some old clothes at the garage sale, anyway. Believe me, this voodoo doll idea is the best one yet. This will really test our skills as witches."

7

In the Dark Attic

It was warm Saturday morning, with barely a breeze to move the branches of the trees. The sun shone brightly on the rust and golden leaves. Pumpkins decorated almost every front porch on Hopper Street. Ben and Buster climbed the oak tree in the cemetery and sat in the crook of the branches. They passed a small telescope between them, peering past the church and across the street to the Greeleys' driveway. Mr. Greeley ran a lawnmower beside the house and into the backyard.

Kelly, Jennifer, and Adelaide sat with their backs against the Geister mausoleum. They looked up as the first customer parked a white car in the driveway and stepped out. Soon a second car pulled up.

Malvina Krebs hurried down the sidewalk with a box of clothes and dumped them onto a card table in the Greeleys' driveway. Mrs. Greeley waved to her. The two of them had become quite good friends ever since Mrs.

Greeley had started coming to Malvina Krebs' Thursday afternoon séances.

"I have a little money," said Kelly. "I could just walk over and look around."

"If we're going to make a real voodoo doll," said Adelaide, "we've got to get some of Rae Jean's old clothes to stick into the doll. We're supposed to have her fingernails and bits of her hair, too, if we really want it to work."

"I don't believe in voodoo," grumbled Jennifer.

"Jennifer! What kind of a witch are you?" asked Kelly. "Voodoo is nothing but black magic. All witches, I mean real witches, believe in magic. You've got to believe!"

"I just don't think it will work."

"Of course it'll work!" Kelly had checked out every book on witchcraft from the school library. "You should see the voodoo dolls they used to make over in Africa. They worked!" She leaned over and whispered, "If we could just find the hair of a hanged man and the dust from a grave to sprinkle on it, I'd be afraid to touch the thing, it would be so powerful."

"And just where are we going to find the hair of a hanged man?" asked Jennifer.

"We'll forget that." Kelly ran her hand across Simon Pedecker's gravestone. "But we sure have dust from a grave."

"I'm not going over there," stated Adelaide, craning her long neck to see the garage-sale activities. "What if Rae Jean asks me why I never showed up last Tuesday to help her with math?"

"I'm not going, either," said Jennifer. She watched as Malvina Krebs sat down with Mrs. Greeley at a small red table. They each held teacups. "Mrs. Greeley yelled at me once for walking on top of their fence. I think she's mean."

"You're all chicken," stated Kelly. She stood up and brushed the leaves from her pants. "I guess I, as the second-power witch, will do the spying."

"If you're a second-power witch, what are we?" asked Adelaide.

"First-power witches. If you learn your chants a little better and quit asking so many questions, I may promote you both to second-power witches." With that, Kelly walked boldly across the cemetery, past the church, across the street, and into the Greeleys' driveway.

"Do you have any girls' sweaters?" a customer asked.

"Oh, that box of sweaters! I do believe I've forgotten to bring them down from the attic," said Mrs. Greeley. She turned around and spotted Kelly. "Kelly! Would you mind helping me bring down a box of clothes from the attic? I think I twisted my back carrying out those chairs. Would you mind? I'll show you where it is." She smiled.

"I can help," said Mrs. Krebs. Kelly looked at Malvina Krebs sitting by the money box and remembered how she had thought Malvina was a witch, just because she looked like a witch with her long, skinny arms, her pointed nose, and her short, black hair. And Malvina certainly believed in ghosts or she wouldn't hold séances in her living room every Thursday afternoon. But Malvina was no witch, Kelly was sure. She was a snoopy, busybody neighbor, but she was definitely not a witch.

"No, no," said Mrs. Greeley. "I really need you to watch the money box and help all the customers, Malvina. Kelly and I can get it. OK, Kelly?"

"Sure!" Kelly followed Mrs. Greeley into the old two-story Victorian house.

"I hope you don't mind," said Mrs. Greeley. "I'd have Rae Jean help, but she went to Susan's this morning."

"I don't mind," answered Kelly. "I just came to look around at your sale." Mrs. Greeley had long black hair and pale blue eyes. She was very pretty, much prettier than Rae Jean. But somehow Kelly felt uncomfortable. There was something mysterious about Mrs. Greeley's smile, something cold about her eyes. Kelly could hardly look at her blue eyes without glancing away.

She looked at all the pictures on the walls as they passed down the hall toward the stairway. Mrs. Greeley was a photographer and traveled all over the world taking pictures of animals and people from faraway lands. There were also several pictures of Rae Jean hanging on the walls.

"I should have sold all these things before we moved here," said Mrs. Greeley. "It's amazing how many things we accumulated over the years." She padded quietly up the stairs, almost as though she were floating. Kelly held on to the rail and followed behind. All she could think about was the voodoo doll and the Halloween party and how much nicer Mrs. Greeley was than Rae Jean. How could such a beautiful mother have such an obnoxious daughter? Did Mrs. Greeley know that Rae Jean had not invited Kelly to the party?

When they reached the second floor, they walked down a hall filled with colorful photographs. There were pictures of African tribesmen, misty lakes, totem poles, decrepit houses, old women with babushkas on their heads, sea gulls, and a large black cat. On seeing the picture of Esmerelda, Kelly turned away quickly. Mrs. Greeley pulled a rope in the hall ceiling and a set of wooden stairs swung down. They climbed the creaking stairs and entered a dark attic. Kelly bumped her head on the low ceiling.

"Do be careful, Kelly," said Mrs. Greeley. She smiled. But her eyes seemed cold. Kelly felt as though they were boring a hole straight through her. She looked down and saw a large wooden box filled with purple candles of all sizes and shapes.

"Where did you get all these candles?"

"Oh, here and there. You might say I'm a candle collector."

Kelly reached for a candle, but suddenly Mrs. Greeley rushed forward and blocked her outstretched arm. "No! Please don't touch these things." She quickly laughed. "Come along, Kelly. Mrs. Krebs is waiting for us. Aha! Here's the box." She pulled a box from the corner and stood up with a groan. "Oh, my back! I simply cannot lift a thing."

Kelly peered into the box. "What a beautiful sweater!" She touched a soft, pink sweater.

"It's angora." Mrs. Greeley pulled the sweater from the box and held it up to Kelly. "Would you like it?"

"Well, I . . . I never had a sweater like this."

"Take it." Mrs. Greeley stood there, tall and straight, holding the pink angora sweater in her hands. Kelly took it.

"Thank you," she said, although she knew she would never wear the sweater. She would never wear anything Rae Jean had worn. After placing the sweater on top of the clothes, she lifted the box and followed Rae Jean's mother out of the musty attic.

Malvina Krebs was busy counting money and making

change. Kelly set the box on a table and tucked the sweater under her arm. She looked around at all the tables. "Does this blow dryer work?" She held up a red plastic hair dryer.

"Sometimes it does and sometimes it doesn't."

Kelly had an idea. With a good blow dryer, some scissors, and a bottle of shampoo, she could open a beauty shop and Rae Jean could be the first customer. Now she knew how she could get a bit of Rae Jean's hair and some fingernail clippings.

"I'll take it." Kelly handed a dollar to Mrs. Greeley and hurried out of the garage just as Rae Jean turned into the driveway on her bicycle.

"Hey! That's my best angora sweater you've got there."

"Your mother gave it to me."

"Mom! You can't give away my angora sweater."

"It's scratchy, Rae Jean. Remember?" Mrs. Greeley whispered to her daughter. But Kelly heard her.

Rae Jean looked at a row of dresses hanging on a pole. "Mom! You can't sell this long dress. I need it for my princess costume. I told you I want to be a princess for Halloween."

Kelly ran down the driveway with the angora sweater under one arm and the blow dryer under the other. At the street, she turned around and called, "Rae Jean, did you hear about our Hopper Street Health Spa?"

"Your what?"

"I'm opening a health spa today at my house. We're having the big grand opening at one o'clock. I thought since you want to be a princess for Halloween, we could give you a fabulous beauty treatment. We do aerobic dance exercises, whirlpool baths, saunas, manicures, facials, shampoos, haircuts, styling, the works! And today only, for our super grand opening, there will be special door prizes. Want to come?"

"Maybe," said Rae Jean, turning her back to Kelly, "if I don't have anything better to do."

Mud Mask
Maneuver

At five minutes to one, the doorbell rang. "It's Rae Jean!" cried Kelly. "I knew she'd come. Hurry!" Jennifer folded towels. Adelaide and Ben taped yellow crepe-paper streamers down the hall and all around the family room. Buster sat on the sofa blowing up balloons. Kelly hung a sign on the bathroom door that said:

HOPPER STREET HEALTH SPA
WELCOME

The girls wore red shorts, white sweatshirts, and leg warmers. Buster and Ben refused to wear anything except jeans and sweatshirts, grand opening or no grand opening.

"Open the door!" called Kelly as she raced to turn on her mother's aerobic dance record. She threw herself onto the plastic mat on the floor and began to do sit-ups. Jennifer and Adelaide joined her, counting—*one, two, three* —to the fast-paced music. Ben and Buster opened the door.

"Want to play catch?" Alex Bradford tossed a baseball into the air. His blond hair shone in the sunlight. Kelly jumped up and peeked around the corner.

"We're having a health spa," said Ben. "But I guess a game of catch could be our exercise program."

"Let's go," said Buster.

"Wait!" Kelly rushed to the door and grabbed Alex's elbow. "Congratulations! You're our very first customer." She handed him a small box wrapped in newspaper comic pages and tied with a ribbon. "You've won the door prize!"

Alex pulled the ribbon, tore off the paper, and opened the box. "Chocolate chip cookies! My favorite." He reached into the box and crammed a cookie into his mouth.

"Take a seat. We'll give you a haircut like you've never had before," said Kelly.

"What for? I don't need a haircut."

"Come on, Alex. How about a whirlpool footbath or a sauna? It will make you feel alive!"

"I already feel alive. I just want to play catch," he said as Kelly and Adelaide pulled him into the bathroom. Kelly turned on the shower full force, filling the room with hot steam.

"Breathe in," Adelaide ordered. "It's great for the lungs." She took off her glasses and breathed in deeply. "Now put your feet in this tub."

"Let me out of here," yelled Alex. He tore open the bathroom door and ran down the hall, scooping up his box of cookies.

"Do you want to play catch or don't you?" he called to Ben.

59

"Sure, we'll play."

"Let me have one of those cookies," said Buster, following Ben and Alex across the porch.

"Just a minute!" yelled Kelly.

"Give us back our cookies," said Adelaide.

"You can't just walk out like this," said Jennifer.

"Is that any way to treat a customer?" Ben shouted back. He grinned and reached into the box for a cookie. Kelly slammed the door.

"There went our cookies," said Jennifer, "after all that work."

"There went our customer," said Kelly.

"Let's go see if there are any cookies left," suggested Adelaide.

"Can you ever stop thinking about food, Adelaide?" grumbled Jennifer.

"You can't exercise on an empty stomach!"

"All this and Rae Jean never showed up," muttered Kelly. "Oh, well, at least we're rid of Ben and Buster." She had no sooner spoken than the doorbell rang. There stood Rae Jean.

"Well, well, well! Step right in to the Hopper Street Health Spa!" said Kelly.

"Wow. Big deal." Rae Jean looked around at the balloons and yellow streamers. "Make this quick. My father is taking Susan and me to McDonald's this afternoon. I have a ticket for a free hamburger and fries, since I had perfect attendance."

"This won't take long," said Kelly. "First, down on the mats, girls." Kelly did sit-ups and push-ups and jumping jacks and every other exercise she could think of to the aerobic dance record.

"Now," said Adelaide, "I'll be your manicurist today." She filled a bowl with warm water, squirted in some pink dish detergent, and pushed Rae Jean's hands into the bowl. While Adelaide held the bowl, Kelly snipped at Rae Jean's long black curls with the scissors.

"Are you sure you know what you're doing?"

"Are you kidding? I spend all my time hanging around Sweetley's Beauty Shop. I'm going to be a professional hairstylist when I grow up."

"Big deal. I'm going to be a famous model for TV commercials. I'm going to be rich."

Kelly scooped up the black curls and dropped them into a bag. She winked at Adelaide. Adelaide dried Rae Jean's hands on a towel and began to clip her fingernails onto a napkin.

"Come into the bathroom, and we'll give you one of our famous shampoos." Rae Jean followed Kelly into the bathroom. Kelly filled the sink with water and pushed Rae Jean's head into the sink. She squirted her mother's seaweed shampoo onto her hair.

"Whew! What smells so funny?" asked Rae Jean.

"This is my mother's expensive seaweed shampoo. She got it from a Japanese import shop. You use this, Rae Jean, and you won't have one gray hair. Not one!"

"I don't have any gray hair, anyway. What do you think I am, ancient or something?"

"Hold still."

"It's burning my eyes!"

Kelly rinsed her hair, blotted it dry with a towel, and turned on the blow dryer she had bought. It rattled and blew warm air at Rae Jean's wet hair for one minute and then stopped. Kelly shook it.

61

"Hey, I want my money back. This dryer doesn't even work."

"Just get my hair dry, would you? I've got to go to McDonald's."

Kelly shook the blow dryer, and it started again. Jennifer carefully scooped a handful of sticky mud from a bucket and slowly smeared it across Rae Jean's face. She worked quickly, spreading the smooth mud across her forehead, under her eyes, over her nose and cheeks, and around her mouth.

"What do you think you're doing?" screamed Rae Jean as she looked into the mirror.

"Keep your mouth closed! Don't talk! Don't say a word!" ordered Jennifer. Rae Jean closed her mouth. "You can't talk when you get a mud mask facial. You'll ruin the effect."

"Is that what this is?" Rae Jean's eyes looked like two white lily pads in a mud puddle as she stared into the mirror. She spit some mud from her mouth. "I look horrible!"

"Of course you do," explained Jennifer. "First you look awful, then you look beautiful. That's how it works. You should see my mother when she gets ready for a party. You wouldn't believe it was the same person. Now don't talk. You'll ruin the mask."

The mud mask began to slide downward and drip onto Rae Jean's sweater.

"This is the biggest mess I've ever seen! Wash it off. I never asked for a stupid mud mash."

"Mask," corrected Jennifer.

"Uh, Jennifer," whispered Kelly, "where did you get this mud mask?"

"I found some good, soft mud in your garden. Why?"

"My mother gets hers from a jar," said Adelaide.

"Oh, no," groaned Rae Jean. "This is worse than the plague! Will this concoction of yours kill me?"

"It's not going to kill you," said Kelly. "Calm down! There's just a little wiggly worm crawling in it. See? Hold still." Rae Jean screamed and splashed water all over her face. "It's only a little worm, Rae Jean. Don't have a fit. If you'll hold still, I'll get it."

"I hate your stupid health spa!" shouted Rae Jean. She grabbed a towel from Jennifer and wiped her muddy face and neck. "You ought to be astronauts when you grow up, all three of you, and fly straight to Pluto and never come back. You should never be in the beauty business!" Rae Jean tried to turn on the hair dryer but couldn't. She threw it on the floor.

"What is your problem?" asked Jennifer.

"I'm not the one with the problem. You're the ones with the problem. If I was as ugly as you, I'd give up. I'd sure get out of the beauty business!" She stomped to the door and slammed it behind her.

"She didn't like the mud mask," said Kelly.

"I thought I was doing a pretty good job." Jennifer wiped her hands on a towel.

"She didn't need to call us ugly." Adelaide looked at herself in the mirror. "Do you think I'm ugly?" She pulled back her shoulders, took off her glasses, and studied her face.

"You're gorgeous, Adelaide," said Kelly.

"I am not. I'm ugly. Rae Jean's right."

"I like you better with your glasses on. You look more like you," said Jennifer.

"Did you get the fingernails?" Kelly asked Adelaide.

Adelaide set her glasses back on her nose and smiled her big, toothy grin. Then she frowned. "I'm not gorgeous at all. You just said that. I hate my nose. Look at it!"

"Adelaide, you look great to me," said Kelly. "You're tall enough to be a glamorous model, you know, or a movie star."

"You're just saying that."

"Where'd you put the fingernails, Adelaide?" asked Kelly.

"They're right here." Adelaide held out the white napkin.

"Perfect! OK, tonight's the night for the voodoo doll. Meet me by the sycamore tree at midnight. We'll do a little voodoo magic."

"Should I bring Boris?" Adelaide asked. "My dog?"

"Bring him. And I'll bring Cinnamon."

"I wish I had a good familiar," said Jennifer. "Every witch needs a good familiar."

"I wish you did, too. We've got to gather all the powers we can for this voodoo spell," said Kelly.

"Did you say midnight?" Jennifer looked worried.

"Midnight is the witching hour. Hee, hee, hee!" Kelly said in her cackling witch voice.

" ' . . . Then you shall be in my power,' " recited Adelaide, remembering the mysterious blue notepaper tacked to the cherry tree.

Voodoo Magic

The mantle clock struck twelve. Kelly quickly climbed out of bed and picked up Ben's violin case and a bag she had placed next to her bed earlier. She tiptoed as quietly as she could up the basement stairs and into the kitchen. She almost dropped the violin when she saw a dark figure sitting at the kitchen table.

"What are you doing with my violin?" whispered Ben. He stuffed a bologna, cheese, salami, lettuce, mustard, and pickle sandwich into his mouth.

"Ben McCoy! What are you doing up?"

"I got hungry."

"I'm telling Dad how you eat all his favorite bologna and rye bread in the middle of the night."

"You do and I'll tell how you sneak out in the middle of the night. Where ya going, anyway—a concert?" asked Ben with his mouth full.

Kelly tried to squeeze past him.

"What's in the bag? Let me see," he asked.

"None of your business."

"What's in the bag?" He grabbed the bag from her hand and peered inside. "What's all this junk?"

Kelly gave up. She couldn't do anything without her brother finding out about it. She took back the bag. "This is valuable stuff. It's everything we need to make a voodoo doll."

"Wow! Tonight?"

"Shhh!"

"And you were going to leave me out?" Ben drank the last of his glass of chocolate milk, wiped his mouth on his sleeve, tied his bathrobe tighter, and said, "OK, I'm ready."

"Wonderful." Kelly put on her jacket, lifted Cinnamon from his box, and carefully opened the back door. Ben followed her through the yard to the clearing in the woods.

"Where have you been?" demanded Adelaide. "I've been waiting for hours." Boris the basset hound sat obediently by her side. He was so old and fat that Kelly wondered how he had ever walked all the way from the Borseman home to the woods. She put Cinnamon down by the hound dog. Boris sniffed the skunk, put his head between his paws, and yawned.

"Where's Jennifer?"

"I don't think she's coming," said Adelaide. "Come on, let's make this voodoo doll. I'm freezing."

"She really should be here," said Kelly as she opened her bag and pulled out the bottle of olive oil. She sprinkled a nine-foot circle of olive oil around the sycamore tree.

"Witches and warlocks, we will now open our meeting. Stand inside the magic circle and say the magic words."

Kelly stepped into the circle and held out her hands. Adelaide and Ben followed. After joining hands, the three began to walk slowly in a circle around the tree, chanting:

Turius, Murius, Zurius! A voodoo doll will grow.
Turius, Murius, Zurius! We'll make it out of dough.

They twirled faster and faster around the tree, kicking their feet in the air and looking up at the branches above them. Finally they dropped to the ground, out of breath.

Kelly pulled the Play Doh from the bag and formed it with her hands. First came the head, then the body, then the arms and legs. "What do you think?" She held it up. "Does it look like Rae Jean?"

"It looks like Rae Jean with a mud mask," said Adelaide. She pressed some of Rae Jean's hair onto the doll's head and stuck fingernails all over it.

Kelly pulled the angora sweater from the bag. "I really hate to cut this up. It's just too beautiful."

"Well, cut the tag from it," said Adelaide. "The one that says 'Made in Korea.'"

"Good idea!" Kelly snipped the tag from the collar of the sweater and pressed it into the doll's stomach. "Did you bring the dust from the grave, like I told you?"

"Right here." Adelaide sprinkled the doll with dust.

"Good! Now, according to an ancient Hungarian legend, the doll must be stuck with pins while a violin plays beautiful music, all under a harvest moon."

"There's the harvest moon," said Adelaide, pointing toward the dark sky.

"I'll play the violin," said Ben. "It's my violin."

"OK, Ben, and I'll stick the doll with toothpicks. I couldn't find any pins."

"Are you sure this isn't dangerous?" asked Adelaide.

Kelly stuck the first toothpick into the voodoo doll. "Did you ever have a mosquito bite?"

"Yeah, but—"

"That's probably how Rae Jean'll feel tomorrow. Like she's covered with mosquito bites, hundreds of them."

"Probably! You mean you don't know for sure? You're putting a voodoo spell on someone and you don't know what crazy things might happen?"

"Keep your voice down, would you? This isn't really going to hurt Rae Jean. We wouldn't do anything that would really hurt. It'll just make her skin itchy or give her a little headache. Nothing to get all excited about."

"That poor doll," said Adelaide. "It's beginning to look like a porcupine."

"Go on, Ben," said Kelly. "We need some beautiful music." Ben lifted his violin to his chin and drew the bow across the strings. Soon the woods were filled with the sound of "Ninety-nine Bottles of Beer on the Wall," one of Ben's favorites.

"Oh, please, Ben," said Adelaide. "Spare me." She clapped her hands over her ears. "She said beautiful music, *beautiful!*"

When Ben hit the E string with his bow, Boris let out with a long, pitiful howl. "Quiet, familiar!" ordered Kelly. But Boris howled again as Ben played another note on the E string. "Can't you make your dog shut up?"

"I can't help it. He always howls when he hears music. You should hear him when my mother sings."

"He'll wake the whole neighborhood!"

"It was your idea to bring him. I never wanted to bring him."

Kelly quickly poked three more toothpicks into the Play Doh doll and held it up. "You can stop, Ben."

Ben stopped playing. Boris stopped howling. "If that didn't raise the dead, I don't know what will." Kelly studied the voodoo doll and said in a eerie-sounding, hushed whisper, "The deed is done. Rae Jean is sure to come down with a case of hives or something. Watch and see."

Adelaide examined the horrible-looking voodoo doll. "I don't like it." She stroked old Boris's head.

"How would you like to be stuck full of toothpicks?" asked Ben.

"Rae Jean isn't stuck full of toothpicks," argued Kelly. "The voodoo doll is. There's a big difference."

"Yeah, but the idea is the same."

"Let's take them out," said Adelaide.

"But the spell won't work if we do that."

"Let's take them out anyway."

"After going to all this trouble?"

"Come on, Kelly," insisted Adelaide.

Kelly held the terrible doll up in the air. "All right," she finally said. "You win. Even Rae Jean doesn't deserve this fate." She pulled out the toothpicks, one by one. "Let her have her dumb party. I don't care."

The Evil Eye

Jennifer was gone all day Sunday, visiting her aunt and uncle in Rising Sun. It wasn't until Monday morning that the three witches were able to talk about the Saturday night esbat. They huddled together on the backseat of the school bus as it wound its way down Bielby Road.

"Gosh, I said I was sorry," repeated Jennifer.

"An esbat is extremely important," Kelly whispered. "All witches must show up for *every* esbat, especially midnight meetings."

"I couldn't help it. I fell asleep. I promise it'll never happen again."

"Good."

"Did you make the voodoo doll?"

"Yeah, and we stuck it full of toothpicks, but it looked really gross."

"We pulled the toothpicks out," said Adelaide.

"Chicken." Jennifer laughed.

"That voodoo doll looked dangerous, Jennifer. You

should have seen it. I rolled it up into a ball and threw it away."

"Threw it away? That's even worse than sticking it with toothpicks. Boy, I'm glad I'm not Rae Jean!"

"Well, I didn't know what else to do with it." Kelly looked out the window and wondered how witches ever got rid of old voodoo dolls. Did they bury them? Or burn them? Some things were impossible to destroy once they were made. Next time, she decided, she would think twice before making something that couldn't be gotten rid of.

She twisted her gold ring around and around on her finger. "Are you wearing your rings?"

"Yes!" said Adelaide and Jennifer together.

"Don't go anywhere without them." Kelly glanced at all the talking and laughing kids on the bus. "You never know what normal-looking person is really an alien in disguise."

"I know what you mean," whispered Adelaide.

"See that girl over there?" Kelly pointed to a small girl who sat quietly, peering out the window. "She could be a programmed robot from Neptune just waiting to invade our planet for all we know!"

They gazed at the small girl. She suddenly turned around and stared at them. The three witches looked down at their feet. Finally Kelly whispered, "Wear your rings. Always! You don't know what danger lurks around every corner!"

The bus stopped at the railroad tracks and then started up again. "I just got a terrific idea!" said Kelly with a snap of her fingers. "Today we'll give Rae Jean the evil eye."

"What's that?" asked Adelaide.

"I read in *Witchcraft and Magic* that witches can make

73

people feel extremely uncomfortable by staring at them. You have to go like this." Kelly turned and looked directly at Jennifer. She pulled her eyebrows together as though she were angry and pinched her eyes into two narrow slits. Then she stared as hard and menacingly as she could, without blinking an eye.

"Stop it," said Jennifer. "You give me the creeps."

"See? That's the whole idea. The evil eye can work wonders. I don't know why I never thought of it before. If we turn the evil eye on Rae Jean, she'll start feeling very uncomfortable, maybe even guilty for having a party and not inviting us. This'll fix her."

"Do you really think it will work?" asked Jennifer.

"It can't fail! With all three of us, that's six evil eyes, all working on Rae Jean. She's bound to feel rotten. It won't hurt her, just make her feel like she's done something terrible. And she has, hasn't she?"

"I can do it," said Adelaide. "Do you think I should take off my glasses?"

"Let's see." Kelly pulled Adelaide's glasses from her nose. Adelaide squeezed her eyes into slits and stared, unblinking.

"Oh, Adelaide, you look horrible!"

"Really? Thanks." Adelaide turned and gave the evil eye to everyone on the bus.

"You're really good, Adelaide," said Jennifer. "Your eyes could freeze water. I swear they could petrify pickles just by looking at them. I'm not kidding!"

"You're just saying that."

"I mean it."

"I can't wait to try it on Rae Jean."

As soon as the bell rang, Mrs. Ludlow studied her attendance sheet and called out names. Finally she said, "Four absences today. I think the old flu bug is floating around again." Mrs. Ludlow always said silly things like that, trying to get a laugh. A few kids in the front row chuckled and grinned, hoping for A's on their spelling test that day.

Mrs. Ludlow cleared her throat and said, "Is everyone ready for Halloween? Only three more days until the ghosts and goblins dance around the graveyards."

The same kids in the front row laughed, including Rae Jean, who raised her hand over her head and waved it frantically.

"Yes, Rae Jean?"

"I'm going to be a princess this year. I've got the most beautiful silver tiara my mother brought back from France, and I have silver slippers to match and a gorgeous silky blue dress with a lacy collar. Of course, my mom says if I have the best costume at my Halloween party, I should give the prize to someone else. I'm going to have the best—"

"I'm going to be a bum," interrupted Alex. "That's the easiest costume to make."

"I'm going to be a robot," said Susan. Kelly looked at Susan and wondered if she really were a robot. You never could tell for sure.

"I'm going to be a witch," said Adelaide proudly. She felt her ring.

"You look like a witch," said Todd.

"You won't even need a costume," added Rae Jean.

"That will be enough, class," said Mrs. Ludlow, tapping

her ruler on her desk. "Let's open our reading books and get out our vocabulary notebooks. And stop the chitchat."

Adelaide turned around and gave Todd the evil eye, but he wasn't looking. She directed her fierce gaze toward Rae Jean. Kelly and Jennifer joined in. Rae Jean glanced up and saw Kelly and Jennifer glaring at her. Then she saw Adelaide. She stuck out her tongue at all three of them. They continued staring, eyes narrowed into slits.

"Kelly," said Mrs. Ludlow, "do you need glasses? I've never noticed you squinting like that. Can't you see the chalkboard?"

Kelly opened her eyes wide. "Oh, yes, yes! I can see it all right. I just . . . The sun hurts my eyes. I have very sensitive eyes." Mrs. Ludlow walked to the windows and pulled the shades lower.

"Thank you, Mrs. Ludlow."

At noon, the class paraded in a line to the cafeteria. Mr. Johnson, the principal, stood in the hall, watching to make sure everyone behaved. When Rae Jean and Susan sat down, Kelly, Jennifer, and Adelaide slid onto the bench directly across from them. All three of them silently ate their lunches as they fixed the evil eye on Rae Jean. They never once looked down at their plates. They just stared at Rae Jean and chewed slowly, feeling their way through their lunches with their forks and fingers.

"What do you know, tacos and carrot sticks," said Rae Jean. "Yuck. I hate tacos. Tomato sauce makes me sick." But she continued to eat her taco. "Are you coming to my party Friday?" she asked Susan.

"Well, I'm not sure," joked Susan. "What if the poison plague gets me?"

"Oh, come on, Susan. There's no such thing as the

poison plague. Some nut wrote those stupid notes. You don't believe that stuff, do you?"

"I guess not."

"My party is going to be fantastic," continued Rae Jean, loudly enough so everyone at the table could hear her. "I'm making a real spooky haunted house in the basement, with sheets and cardboard boxes. And there'll be peeled grapes for eyeballs and wet spaghetti noodles for dead man's brains and—"

"Shhh!" said Susan. "You're giving away all the surprises."

"You're right. You'll just have to come and see for yourself. Want my cookie, Alex? I hate peanut butter cookies." Rae Jean passed her cookie over to Alex with a big smile on her face.

"Thanks," said Alex. He swallowed the cookie in one gulp.

"You should see the fantastic decorations my mother is fixing. It's going to be a super party. We'll have a blast!"

"If the poison plague doesn't get us first," warned Todd.

Rae Jean ignored him. "And we'll dunk for apples and tell ghost stories and everything. My mother is even making spicy doughnuts, and she's putting a surprise inside one of them."

"A surprise?" asked Todd.

"That's right. Whoever gets the lucky doughnut will get a very expensive surprise." Everyone at the table began talking at once about the Halloween party.

Rae Jean looked at Kelly, Jennifer, and Adelaide. They continued to fix the evil eye gaze on her without saying a word. Kelly picked up a carrot stick and bit off the end.

"What's the matter with you, anyway?" asked Rae

Jean. "Why don't you bring a camera and take a picture?" Kelly, Jennifer, and Adelaide chewed carrots and continued to stare.

"Can't you talk?" shouted Rae Jean. "You've been staring at me all day, and I'm sick of it. Why don't you go stare at a mirror? Oh, no, don't do that. You might crack it." She looked at Susan, and they laughed and began to whisper, looking up every now and then at Kelly.

"Did you hear about Kelly's stupid health spa?" Rae Jean asked Susan. "Believe me, don't ever go. I'm warning you, Susan!" She laughed. "Now I know why they're so ugly. They wash their hair in stinky seaweed and plaster their faces with wormy mud mash!"

"Mud *mask*," corrected Kelly.

"That's what I said, birdbrain. Hey, I thought you couldn't talk. We thought you were too dumb to talk, didn't we?" Rae Jean punched Susan on the shoulder.

Kelly glared at Rae Jean. "Quit staring at me, would you? You're ruining my appetite." Rae Jean suddenly picked up her half-eaten taco and flung it onto Kelly's plate. Taco sauce spattered onto Kelly's blouse. "There! How do you like that, smelly Kelly? Smelly, smelly Kelly. Fat belly Kelly."

The bell rang, and Kelly ran to the rest room on the way back to class. She washed the taco sauce from her blouse and quickly returned to her seat in Room 19.

Later that afternoon, Todd's mother walked into the classroom and placed a white box on Mrs. Ludlow's desk. After she left, Mrs. Ludlow announced, "Today is Todd's birthday." Everyone sang "Happy Birthday" while Todd blushed.

"Todd, would you like to pass out the ice cream to the class?" Todd walked from desk to desk, dropping a little round container of ice cream and a wooden spoon onto each desk.

"Strawberry!" wailed Rae Jean as she pulled the lid from her container.

"What's wrong?" asked Mrs. Ludlow.

"I'm allergic to strawberries. I break out in splotches and get dizzy and everything."

"Well, Rae Jean, I guess someone else will have to eat your share." Rae Jean looked longingly at her ice cream. She had hardly eaten any of her lunch.

"I'll eat your ice cream!" called Adelaide. She reached for Rae Jean's container.

"I'll eat it!" screeched Rae Jean. She dug her spoon into the strawberry ice cream. "I wouldn't give you my ice cream for a million dollars."

It wasn't long after snack time that Rae Jean got sick. Kelly, Jennifer, and Adelaide all watched as she walked to Mrs. Ludlow's desk. "I have a terrible headache, Mrs. Ludlow. And my stomach hurts, too."

"I bet it's that old flu bug floating around again," said Mrs. Ludlow with a sigh.

"No, it's that crummy strawberry ice cream. I can't eat strawberries. Why couldn't she bring vanilla ice cream? Oh, Mrs. Ludlow, I've got to go home. Right now!"

"Go down to the nurse," said Mrs. Ludlow. A minute later, Patty and Matt went up to Mrs. Ludlow's desk. "I feel sick," said Matt. "My stomach hurts. Can I go home?"

"Feel my face," said Patty. "I'm burning up."

Mrs. Ludlow looked undecided. She felt Patty's forehead. "Why is it when one person gets sent to the nurse's office, everyone wants to go? It's like an epidemic."

"It's the poison plague," said Alex.

"We're all getting the plague! I knew it!" cried Susan.

"Now, class, settle down!" ordered Mrs. Ludlow, but nobody settled down after Rae Jean, Patty, and Matt left to go home. If those three had been struck with the plague, who would be next?

11
Dead Man's Hand

On Wednesday, Adelaide pulled old Boris across the yard all the way to the sycamore tree in the woods. She carried her broom in her other hand.

"Hurry up, Adelaide. We've been waiting for at least an hour. What took you so long?" Kelly stroked Cinnamon's silky black-and-white fur.

"You'd go slow, too, if you had to drag Boris all the way down the street. He was taking a nap." She patted the basset hound on his head.

"Burying that rabbit's foot must have really helped our powers," said Jennifer. "I'm beginning to think we're genuine witches!" She planted her broom, handle down, and began to dance around it.

"Did you ever think we weren't?" asked Kelly. "You've got to believe, Jen, if you want anything to work."

"Boy, Rae Jean really was hit with the plague the other day," said Adelaide.

"It was the voodoo doll," said Kelly. "She was OK

today. That voodoo doll hex must have worked after all. We've got to be careful with all the magical powers we're gaining."

"Of course, it might have been the strawberry ice cream," said Jennifer. "Or the taco. Or the old flu bug floating around."

Kelly gave Jennifer a sharp look. "It was the voodoo doll. That thing was dangerous. We never should have made it."

"I think you're right," agreed Adelaide.

"Maybe," mumbled Jennifer.

"Here it is, only two days from Halloween, and we three witches haven't cast a single spell on Rae Jean's party. We've got to think of something," said Kelly. "But first I shall call this esbat to order."

She opened a bag, pulled out a long black dress, and slipped it on. She tied the middle with an old rope. Then she took off her tennis shoes and put on a pair of black, high-heeled shoes. On her head, she placed a pointed hat with scraggly, gray hair hanging all around the edges.

"Heh, heh, heh, heh!" she cackled.

"I love it!" said Jennifer. "Where did you get such a good costume?"

"I found the shoes and dress in a box in the basement. You can find anything in our basement if you look long enough. The hat I got at Murphy's. Isn't it terrific?"

"It sure is," said Adelaide.

"Now, my witches, gather inside the magic circle, and we shall dance by the light of the moon."

"What moon? It's not dark yet," said Jennifer.

"Your imagination needs a lot of work, Jenny. Gather around!"

The three witches of Hopper Street danced and sang and waved their brooms around the sycamore tree. "This is the seventh day, time to test our brooms for the great flight on Halloween night," said Kelly in her most witch-like voice. In her costume, she felt like a true witch.

"What flight?" asked Adelaide.

"Our broom flight over Lawrenceburg, over Aurora, over all of Indiana. We're going to the grand esbat held every year in the great city of Cleveland!"

"On these dirty old brooms?" asked Adelaide.

"Dirty old brooms? Adelaide! These magical brooms have been greased with the fat of newborn piglets, belladonna, and soot. They are no longer your ordinary brooms!"

"I forgot."

"Now, sit on your broom and prepare for flight," ordered Kelly, straddling her broom. "Close your eyes and repeat the magic words, 'Turius, Murius, Zurius, these are brooms most curious.'"

Turius, Murius, Zurius,
These are brooms most curious.

The three witches chanted the magic words over and over. Finally they stopped. The woods were silent except for the rustling of leaves in the chilly breeze.

"I wonder why it isn't working," said Adelaide.

"I think I know," said Kelly. "Remember? The book said the fat of a newborn piglet. That bacon we used was probably some old pig or something. Maybe it was even that artificial stuff. Our ingredients just weren't right. You can only substitute so much." She tossed her broom to the ground and plopped into the pile of leaves.

"I didn't want to fly anywhere anyway," said Jennifer, "especially not Cleveland."

"What's wrong with Cleveland? My uncle lives in Cleveland," said Adelaide, dropping her broom to the ground and wiping her hands on her jeans.

"What we need to do," said Kelly, suddenly jumping up from the leaf pile, "is scare Rae Jean! We'll scare her so bad, she'll never want to see a Halloween ghost or goblin again."

"And how do you suggest we do that?" asked Adelaide.

Kelly snapped her fingers. "Easy! We'll make a Hand of Glory and leave it on her front doorstep. That will petrify her!"

"What are you talking about?"

"A Hand of Glory. All it is is a dried-out human hand from a corpse. It's guaranteed to strike fear into anyone who sees it. I read all about it in one of my library books."

"A dried out corpse?"

"Sure. I read about this old man who lived in New York City in a really bad neighborhood where prowlers roamed around at night. Well, this old man got himself a Hand of Glory and hung it on his doorknob. Just about every house on his street was burglarized, but not his. Nobody dared touch his door with a Hand of Glory hanging on the doorknob."

"That's gross!" said Jennifer.

"Where did that old man ever find a real dead man's hand?" asked Adelaide.

"He probably dug up a dead man right out of the cemetery, how else?" explained Kelly.

"How did he get his hand?" asked Adelaide.

"That does it, I'm going." Jennifer stood up to go.

Kelly suddenly felt a hand on her back. It slowly slid upward until it gripped her shoulder. She screamed as she spun around and saw a dark figure in a long hooded robe.

"Boy, did I get you!" Ben laughed. Buster crept out of the woods and stood beside him. "How do you like these warlock costumes? We've been working on 'em all afternoon."

"They're scary. Real scary!" Kelly's heart was still pounding. "You didn't need to scare the socks off me though, did you?"

"That's what you're planning to do to Rae Jean," said Ben. "We heard everything."

Buster dropped to a spot next to the sycamore tree and began to dig with a stick in the ground. "What are you doing, Buster? Digging up a corpse?" asked Kelly.

"I'm getting my rabbit's foot back, that's what. I got a D today on my social studies test, and it's all because I didn't have my lucky rabbit's foot." He pulled the rabbit's foot from the ground and shook the dirt from it.

" 'To gain magical energy and strengthen one's powers as a witch, one must bury a good luck charm by the light of the moon,' " chanted Kelly.

"Do you really think our powers are strengthened?" asked Jennifer.

"It sure didn't help me on my social studies test," grumbled Buster. He stuck the rabbit's foot in the large pocket of his father's old brown bathrobe.

"We are not concentrating enough, that's our number one problem," explained Kelly. "Witches and warlocks, gather around the circle!" Kelly reached for Adelaide's and Jennifer's hands. "Everyone hold hands like this and close your eyes. OK, now think!"

"About what?" asked Buster, opening his eyes.

"About how we can get a good Hand of Glory to hang on Rae Jean's doorknob."

"And we'll stick a note between the fingers saying the poison plague is coming to anyone who gives a party on Halloween night!"

"That's good, Ben," said Kelly.

"I have an old rubber glove we could fill with Jell-O," suggested Jennifer.

"Wait!" called Buster. The children opened their eyes and looked at him. "I bought one of those scary monster hands at Murphy's last year. It really looks ugly."

"We'll fill it with Jell-O, cherry Jell-O," said Kelly, "and when the Jell-O starts to melt, it'll look like blood dripping out of the wrist."

"Oh, yuck!" said Jennifer.

"That sounds good," said Ben. "I'll make the Jell-O."

"I'll write the note!" said Adelaide.

"Great! Meet here tomorrow, just as the sun is going down, and we'll make the Hand of Glory," said Kelly.

At seven o'clock the next evening, the witches and warlocks of Hopper Street met once again by the campfire in the woods. Buster held out the monster hand as Ben poured the Jell-O into it. Kelly tied the wrist with white adhesive tape, leaving a small opening for the Jell-O to drip out.

"Just in case it's not gruesome enough, I brought some ketchup," said Adelaide. She shook a blob of ketchup onto the back of the hairy-looking hand and smeared it around.

"I thought this was supposed to be dried out," said Jennifer.

"This is worse," said Kelly. She picked up the slippery hand and tossed it to the ground. Everyone jumped back and stared at the monster hand which lay on the ground near a rock. It almost seemed, there in the growing darkness, that the ground was opening and a dead man was struggling out of his grave, his hand grasping for the rock.

"Get it!" yelled Kelly.

"Are you kidding?" cried Jennifer.

Ben scooped up the monster hand, and the five of them ran from the gloomy woods, cutting across backyards until they reached the cemetery. Long, dark shadows stretched across the rows of gravestones. The children crouched in the shadows of the Geister tomb and peeked around it toward the Greeley house across the street. A lamp had just been turned on in the front window. Another light was turned on upstairs.

"I'm not going over there!" said Jennifer.

"You are so chicken, you really are," said Kelly.

"Well, if you're so brave, you go! This is all your crazy idea anyway."

"What if Mrs. Greeley catches us and yells at us?" asked Adelaide.

"No one's going to catch us," said Kelly.

Boris finally caught up with the group. The old dog slowly sat down and began to howl. "What's he howling about now?" asked Kelly.

"He always howls at the moon," explained Adelaide.

"What doesn't he howl at? They're going to hear us!"

"I'll take the hand over," said Buster. He took the wobbly hand from Ben. "But shut up Boris, OK?"

Adelaide held Boris's jaws closed while Buster crept across the street. He draped the Hand of Glory on the doorknob and pressed the doorbell. Then he raced as fast as he could back across the street and slid to the ground behind the granite mausoleum, like a baseball player diving into home plate.

Slowly they peeked around the tomb and watched as Rae Jean opened her front door.

12

Gypsy Love Potion

The next day was Halloween. The huge moon was rising above the branches of the trees as Kelly, Ben, and Samantha rushed about the house putting the finishing touches on their costumes. Dr. McCoy sat in his favorite recliner, reading the *Register*. Mrs. McCoy carefully watered her African violets on the marble-top table.

"I don't understand what has happened to my poor dieffenbachia plant," she said. "Look at this, Stan. It seems to be losing its leaves." Dr. McCoy peered over the top of his paper.

"Too much water," he said simply.

"I'm not watering it that much. Do you suppose it's getting too much fertilizer?"

"Oh, I know, Mom," yelled Ben, but Kelly quickly interrupted him.

"We're holding our grand esbat tonight, out in the front yard," she announced, shooting a warning look toward Ben.

"A grand what?" asked Mrs. McCoy, still puzzling over the scraggly dieffenbachia plant.

"Our witch meeting. This is the biggest one of the year," explained Kelly. "Do you think Jennifer and Adelaide and I could pass out the candy this year? We'll put it in our witches' cauldron. The kids will love it."

"You mean, I won't have to answer the doorbell all night long?" asked Kelly's father with a smile.

"Right, Dad. We witches will hand out the candy. You won't be bothered at all."

"That sounds good to me," answered Dr. McCoy. He turned a page of the paper.

"Come on," yelled Samantha. She danced about in her clown costume. "Everyone's coming. Let's go, Ben!"

"I'm not going with *you*. You go too slow." Ben snatched his plastic pumpkin and ran for the front door.

"I want to go with you," wailed Samantha. "I'm not going by myself. Mom!"

"Go with Marigold," called Ben, opening the door.

"No!" cried Samantha, with a frown on her red-spotted clown face. "Dad!"

"Take your sister with you, Ben," said Dr. McCoy.

"Aw, Dad. I always get stuck with her. Let Kelly take her."

"Not me," said Kelly. "I'm holding a witch meeting in the front yard." Ben groaned and went out the front door. Samantha picked up her plastic pumpkin and ran along behind him.

Kelly quickly ran to the sycamore tree in the woods. Jennifer and Adelaide were already there, dressed in long black dresses and black witches' hats. Together the three witches carried the old camping pot to the McCoys' front yard. They filled it with candy kisses and Snickers bars, and stood huddled around the pot, heads touching. They held their brooms in their left hands and began to sway left and right, cackling and laughing as mysteriously as they could.

Three little ghosts walked up the driveway. "Step right over here, little ghosts, heh, heh, heh!" cackled Kelly. She stirred the candy around and around in the cauldron, swaying slowly forward and backward. The tallest ghost pushed the two smaller ghosts up to the cauldron.

"I am Madame Venezuela and these are my two helpers, Lady LaChoy and Gypsy Jezabubble." Adelaide and Jennifer murmured some strange, foreign-sounding words and danced around their broomsticks.

"Trick or treat," said the tallest ghost.

"Madame Venezuela will stand for no tricks!" screeched Kelly. "A treat you shall have." She continued stirring the pot with a long spoon. "Turius, Murius, Zurius. Madame Venezuela has special treats tonight. Eye of toad and wing of bat, heart of goat and tail of cat!"

"Don't you have any plain candy?" asked the tallest ghost. The two smaller ghosts held out their bags.

Kelly reached into the pot and pulled out three Snickers bars. She dropped them into their bags. "Heart of goat for you, eye of toad for you, and tail of cat for you!" she cackled. The three ghosts looked into their bags, turned around, and ran down the driveway.

"That was great!" said Jennifer. "This is fun!"

"Let me hand out the next treat," said Adelaide.

"My powers are failing me," cried Kelly as she held the back of her hand to her forehead. "Witches! Are you wearing your enchanted rings?" Jennifer and Adelaide held out their hands to Kelly, and the three rings touched. "We need our familiars. That's what's missing."

"Oh, do I have to get Boris?" asked Adelaide.

"Gypsy Jezabubble, go get your dog! We need *all* our powers tonight on this spooky Halloween." Kelly glanced about the shadowy yard, pretending to be filled with fear. "I must get my trusty skunk." She turned toward the front porch.

"I hate that name, Lady LaChoy," complained Jennifer. "Why can't I be Madame Venezuela?"

"Too bad. I thought of it first, Jen," said Kelly. "Gosh, can't you ever go along with anything? Now, please, stir the pot until I get back." Kelly and Adelaide ran off in the darkness and soon returned with Cinnamon and Boris.

"What's that?" asked a little boy dressed in a mouse suit.

Kelly held up Cinnamon. "My name is Madame Venezuela and this is my dog, Cinnamon."

"That doesn't look like any dog I've ever seen," said the mouse.

"That's because this is a very rare dog—a genuine black-and-white ratdog all the way from South America. He is a cross between a South American black rat and a white terrier."

"No kidding! It looks sort of like a skunk to me."

Kelly gasped. "Do not call my dog a skunk! He may *bite* you!"

Adelaide chanted, "Eye of toad and wing of bat, heart of goat and tail of cat." She dropped some candy kisses into the mouse's bag, and he ran away.

"You know," said Kelly, suddenly losing her witch cackle, "I'm really worried about that strange note we found on the tree." She pulled from her pocket the blue stationery with the yellow buttercup in the corner and switched on a flashlight she had brought with her. Pointing the small beam of light toward the paper, she read again:

> Midnight is the witching hour.
> Then you shall be in my power.

"Who could have written this?"

"Well, I know it wasn't me," said Jennifer.

"You don't suppose tonight is the night the note is talking about, do you?" asked Adelaide.

"That's what I'm afraid of. After all, Halloween at midnight is the spookiest, witchiest time of the whole year," said Kelly.

"You know what I read?" Adelaide pushed her pointed hat straight on her head. "I read that if you want to meet a real witch, I mean a *real* witch, you have to put your clothes on wrong side out and walk backward to a crossroads on Halloween night. If you wait 'til the clock strikes twelve, you will see an honest-to-goodness, real live witch."

"Really?" said Kelly.

"Well, count me out," said Jennifer.

"Oh, come on, Jen," said Kelly. "You never want to do anything."

"All right, all right, I'll go. But tonight's the last time. My mother is going to catch me sneaking outside at midnight one of these nights."

"I think it's fun," said Adelaide.

"Shhh!" warned Kelly. A car turned into Rae Jean's driveway. Three bums jumped out.

"There goes Alex," said Kelly.

"And Matt and Todd. Looks like the party's about to begin," said Jennifer.

"Without us." Kelly handed out two more Snickers bars, to a ballerina and a hunchback.

"Hmmm." Adelaide held the flashlight close to the pages of *Spells and Hexes*. "I never knew this!"

"What?"

"Listen to this." She read:

> *Nectar from the flower, honey from the bee,*
> *In his eyes, true love you will see.*

"A love potion!" cried Kelly. "Now, that's what we could use." She watched as Rae Jean opened her front door and Alex, Matt, and Todd walked inside. Another car pulled into the Greeley driveway.

"A genuine witch's love potion!" Kelly's voice rose with excitement. "We three witches will brew up a batch—"

"And take it over to Rae Jean's party—" interrupted Jennifer, catching the excitement.

"And dump it in the cider!" added Adelaide, looking quite pleased with the idea.

"See? Now, *that's* white magic," said Kelly. "We'll be using our powers to do good. We'll bring a little love into the world."

"We won't ruin the party or anything," said Jennifer.

"There's only one small problem," said Adelaide. "We're not invited. Remember?"

"We'll get invited! I have a plan," whispered Kelly. "If you can't beat 'em, join 'em."

"Are we really going to make a love potion?" asked Adelaide.

"Well, it sure sounds easy enough!" said Kelly. "I saw a jar of honey in our kitchen."

"Sure, but where can you find nectar from a flower?" asked Jennifer. "This is October. There aren't any flowers."

"Apricot nectar!" said Adelaide. "We've got some at home. We'll mix it with the honey."

"Come on, witches," said Kelly as she dragged the pot of candy to her front door. "It's time we perked up the party. Gypsy Jezabubble, go get your apricot nectar and meet us here in ten minutes. Lady LaChoy, come with me!"

"I hate that name, Lady LaChoy," grumbled Jennifer. "I don't know, it sounds . . . Chinese for some reason. Whoever heard of a Chinese fortune-teller, anyway?"

"Chinese are famous fortune-tellers. Haven't you ever heard of Confucius?"

"Yes, but—"

"Quit complaining, Jennifer," spoke up Adelaide. "How would you like to be Gypsy Jezabubble? Huh?" Adelaide turned to go when suddenly a small black cat crossed in front of her and disappeared into the bushes.

"A black cat crossed my path," she whispered.

"On Halloween night," said Jennifer.

"That's not a good sign." Kelly shook her head.

13

Madame Venezuela, Lady LaChoy, Gypsy Jezabubble, and the Crystal Ball

Adelaide held Boris by his leash while Jennifer held Cinnamon in her arms. They both stood on tiptoe, peering over Kelly's shoulder. Kelly carefully poured a small jar of honey into a plastic container full of apricot juice. "Nectar from the flower, honey from the bee. Want a sip?" She poured a little into a cup and handed it to Adelaide.

Adelaide drank the whole cup. "Mmmm!"

"You just drank a genuine love potion brewed by a second-power witch, Adelaide."

"Nectar from the flower," argued Jennifer. "Apricots are not flowers."

"Didn't you ever see an apricot tree in bloom?" asked Kelly. "Here, Jennifer, have some." Kelly poured two glasses for herself and Jennifer, and they both drank the sweet potion in silence.

"We should have thought of this a long time ago," said Kelly. She held the plastic container up, closed her eyes, and slowly said in her most mysterious voice, "Madame

Venezuela hereby decrees: Whoever drinks the nectar of the flower and the honey of the bee will forever be in love with . . . ME!"

"Wait a minute," said Adelaide.

"How about us?" spoke up Jennifer.

Kelly opened one eye and closed it again. ". . . will forever be in love with Lady LaChoy, Gypsy Jezabubble, and Madame Venezuela!"

"That's better," said Adelaide.

"How could anybody love someone with a crazy name like Lady LaChoy?" muttered Jennifer.

"Here's the plan," said Kelly. "We'll get into Rae Jean's party as fortune-tellers. And we can use this old fishbowl for a crystal ball. While I'm telling fortunes, you, Gypsy Jezabubble, must somehow dump the love potion into the punch bowl. Do you think you can do it?"

"A witch can do anything." Adelaide smiled.

"So we're not going to ruin good ol' Rae Jean's party?" asked Jennifer.

"What's the use?" answered Kelly. "Everybody's over there having a great time, and we're sitting here like . . . like . . ."

"Like three grumpy old witches," said Adelaide.

"But I can't stand Rae Jean," said Jennifer. "She brags too much."

"That's for sure. But I want to go to the party, not sit around here all night. Everyone's there."

"Everyone like Alex Bradford, you mean." Jennifer poked Kelly's shoulder.

"Oh, Kelly!" Mrs. McCoy walked into the kitchen holding a tattered old cookbook. "You haven't seen my parsley, have you? I've been looking all over the place for it. I wanted to try this new lasagna recipe." She opened a cabinet and began once again to search through the spice cans.

"That's the stuff we rubbed all over our skin, remember?" said Adelaide too quickly.

"Adelaide!"

Mrs. McCoy looked puzzled. "You rubbed parsley all over your skin?"

"Well, Mom, you know how you put all that stuff on your face? You know, the cucumber cream and the coconut oil? We sort of thought parsley flakes might be good for our skin. Doesn't parsley have a lot of vitamin A?"

"I'm not sure," said Mrs. McCoy.

"We'll buy another can of parsley for you, Mrs. McCoy," said Adelaide, "for your lasagna."

"Oh, you don't have to."

"You make the best lasagna," added Jennifer.

"Thank you."

"We're on our way to Rae Jean's Halloween party. She's having a big party tonight, and we don't want to be late."

"I didn't know you were invited to a Halloween party."

"We will be in a few minutes. See you later, Mom."

Kelly hurried to the basement to search for some cloth, a basket, and a small table.

The three witches pressed Rae Jean's doorbell. "A true witch always keeps her familiar with her in case she needs more power!" Kelly put her skunk into the basket and snapped the lid shut.

"Boris is staying out here," said Adelaide. "Sit!" she

ordered. Boris wagged his tail and sat on the porch. "Now, stay!"

The front door suddenly opened wide. Mrs. Greeley stood there staring down at the three witches. With witch hats and scraggly hair and gray faces, it was hard for her to tell exactly who they were.

"Allow me to introduce myself," said Kelly in her mysterious gypsy accent. "I am zee great Madame Venezuela, and my two friends here are Lady LaChoy and Gypsy Jezabubble. Fortune-telling is our trade, and we would take gr-r-reat pleasure in entertaining your guests with genuine predictions of the future. We read palms and tell fortunes. For your special party, we will perform and prophesy for absolutely nothing. Free! Eez that not correct?" She turned around to face Jennifer and Adelaide, who crouched behind her.

Mrs. Greeley laughed. "Come on in, ladies. The party could use some entertainment."

"Thank you ver-r-ry much," said Kelly, rolling her *r*'s as much as she could. She continued to babble on with foreign-sounding words as she and Jennifer and Adelaide quickly threw a black cloth over their little fold-up table. Kelly turned the fishbowl upside down and spread her fingers around it, closing her eyes, lifting her face upward, and mumbling incoherent chants. The three girls held their heads close together.

"What are you doing here?" asked Rae Jean. She carefully stepped around a tub filled with water and floating apples. "I never invited you guys!"

"We are famous gypsies come all zee way from Hunga-r-r-r-y," said Kelly. She looked at the ceiling, closed her eyes again, and rubbed the crystal ball.

101

"Sure you are," sneered Rae Jean.

"And who shall be first to have his fortune told by zee world famous Madame Venezuela? Hmmm? Madame Venezuela eez getting ver-r-r-y impatient!"

As everyone began to gather around the fortune-teller's table, Adelaide slowly backed up with the plastic container holding the carefully concocted love potion. She inched her way to the kitchen table. While no one was looking, she poured the love potion into the punch bowl. She picked up an orange pumpkin-shaped cookie and was about to bite into it when she saw a piece of blue stationery lying on the corner of the kitchen counter.

Adelaide pushed her glasses closer to her eyes, bent over, and closely examined the blue paper. It was the very same paper on which the mysterious note had been written, the note found tacked to the cherry tree. She examined the little yellow flower in the upper left corner of the paper and felt a chill up her spine as she remembered the words of the note:

> Midnight is the witching hour.
> Then you shall be in my power.

Kelly and Jennifer were busy telling fortunes. Kelly reached out and took Alex's hand. "And you, my young man," she said in her mysterious voice, "I see you will be r-r-rich and famous someday!"

"Really?" Alex laughed.

"Do not laugh at Madame Venezuela!" scolded Kelly with a serious look on her face. She peered deeply into the fishbowl. "I see much money in your future, ah, yes, and a beautiful, *beautiful* woman." All the girls began to laugh, and Alex sat down on a chair to get a closer look at the crystal ball.

"I see a large . . . oh dear . . . a large hospital—"

"Oh, no!" cried Patty.

"Have no fear," continued Kelly. "I see this handsome young man as a skillful brain surgeon operating on a famous movie star. He will be paid millions of dollars and will have his name in zee newspapers!"

"Hey, this fortune-teller isn't bad," said Alex.

"Come on, Alex," said Rae Jean, "let's get some more cider."

"Ah, yes! More cider. A ver-r-ry good idea." Kelly glanced at Adelaide, who held up the empty plastic container and winked.

"Drink lots of cider, young man, and bring me a cup. Madame Venezuela is ver-r-ry thirsty."

"It's my turn," said Jennifer. She reached for the fishbowl.

As Jennifer began to chant and mumble fantastic predictions about the future, Adelaide grabbed Kelly's shoulder. Kelly saw a strange look on Adelaide's face. "What's the matter?" Adelaide showed Kelly the piece of blue stationery she had found.

"What do you think of this?"

Kelly studied the paper. "I think Rae Jean did write that note, after all. She was just trying to scare us."

Adelaide looked relieved. "Well, I'm glad it was her and not . . . not a real witch." The two girls looked at Rae Jean who stood by the punch bowl talking to Alex and Matt and Susan.

"How do we know Rae Jean isn't a real witch?"

"Oh, come on."

"You never know."

"Look at that," said Adelaide, pointing to a box in the corner of the kitchen. "There's that little black cat."

Kelly went over to look at the sleeping cat. "It looks just like the one we saw in my front yard."

"The cat is very sick," said Mrs. Greeley. She seemed to have appeared out of nowhere. "She came to our back door a short time ago. Please don't touch her."

Kelly and Adelaide shrank back from the cat. Mrs. Greeley picked up a tray of cookies and disappeared into the crowded family room.

"The poor thing," said Kelly. Cinnamon clawed and scratched inside his basket. Kelly sat down on a kitchen chair and unhooked the basket latch. The skunk climbed out and dropped to the floor, where he waddled quickly under the table.

"Come back here, Cinnamon." Kelly tried to grab her skunk, but it was too late.

"A skunk!" screamed Susan. She stood in the doorway. "There's a skunk under the table!"

Everyone came running. When they saw Cinnamon scurrying around between the chair legs, every ghost, goblin, bum, robot, and princess began to run left and right, bumping into one another and screaming, "Skunk! Skunk! Let's get out of here. Help!"

There was a mad dash to the front door as everyone poured out into the chilly October night. Kelly, Jennifer, and Adelaide ran outside with the rest of them. "Wait!" Kelly called. "He can't hurt anything." But everyone was hollering and screaming.

"I can't believe it," cried Rae Jean. "A real skunk, right in my own kitchen!"

"How did he get in?" asked Patty.

"The question is, How do you get him out?" said Todd. "He'll stink up your whole house if he lets go. I'm talking sewer city!"

"You'll have to move," said Amanda.

Suddenly Boris lifted his head and howled. "Whose dog?" asked Alex.

"Mine," answered Adelaide. "He loves to howl at the moon." She patted Boris's head. "You can stop now, Boris."

"He's harmless," said Kelly.

"Who?" asked Alex. "Boris?"

"No, my skunk. My pet skunk. He can't hurt a thing."

"Kelly!" Adelaide grabbed Kelly's arm.

"You mean that's *your* skunk in my house?" cried Rae Jean.

Kelly laughed. "He's my fam . . . my pet. He's been deodorized."

"Your pet skunk? Whoever heard of having a skunk for a pet?" asked Rae Jean.

"Are you crazy?" said Susan.

"Madame Venezuela has a pet skunk, and he is perfectly harmless. I never go anywhere without him. I just hope I can find him." She looked at Rae Jean. "My skunk is extremely valuable. One of a kind."

"Sure he is," answered Rae Jean. "Just get him out of my house."

All the children slowly followed Kelly back into the house. They walked from room to room, looking under chairs, in closets, behind the sofa, behind the drapes. "You really have a pet skunk?" Alex asked as he lifted a pillow on the sofa and looked underneath.

"I sure do. His name is Cinnamon." Kelly looked up at Alex. He had on a baggy pair of pants with a red patch on the knee, a tattered sweatshirt, a floppy hat, and brown powder streaked across his face. She smiled.

"I guess our love potion didn't work," she said.

"What love potion?" asked Alex.

"The love potion Adelaide poured into the punch bowl."

"You're kidding! I must've drunk a gallon of the stuff."

"Really?"

"Really. Do you think I'll get sick?"

"Not sick, stupid. You'll just fall madly in love."

"With who?"

"I don't know. How should I know?" Kelly's face was burning.

"I think I know."

"You do? Who?"

"With you." Alex suddenly leaned forward and kissed Kelly's cheek. His floppy hat fell off, and he picked it up and walked away.

Rae Jean stood in the doorway, watching her. Cinnamon squirmed in her arms. "Here's your dumb skunk." She pushed Cinnamon into Kelly's arms, turned, and walked away.

"Wait a minute, Rae Jean," called Kelly.

"What?" snapped Rae Jean, spinning around.

Kelly felt her face turning red. She did not want to say what she was about to say. She stroked Cinnamon's fur over and over.

"Hey, there's the skunk!" yelled Patty. She looked up from a stack of tape cassettes.

"Are you sure he's safe?" asked Matt. "Something smells funny."

"He's OK," said Kelly. "Don't worry." Patty and Matt turned back to the tapes. They picked one, pushed it into the tape player, and turned it on full blast. Everyone gathered around the tape player.

Kelly turned back to Rae Jean. "I'm sorry."

"For what?"

"For trying to ruin your party. It was me. I was the one who sent all those notes to everyone."

"I know that."

"You do?"

"I figured it out," said Rae Jean. "It didn't stop anyone from coming, did it?"

Kelly bit her thumbnail. She had said enough. She had said she was sorry, and she meant it. But Rae Jean stood there looking at her, waiting. She decided to tell her a little more. "What did you think of that bloody dead man's hand? We did that, too."

"I thought so. So the poison plague is going to get me, huh? You didn't scare me, Kelly McCoy."

"Well, I wanted to!"

"Why?"

"Because you didn't invite us."

"I never thought you wanted to come, you or Jennifer. Or Adelaide for that matter."

"Well, you thought wrong. I don't like being left out. Do you know how it feels to be left out?"

"Do I know how it feels to be left out? Ha!" Rae Jean plopped onto a chair. "I know exactly how it feels to be

108

left out. It's the way I felt the day you had your big birthday party and didn't even invite me. Remember last July, right after I moved in?"

Kelly didn't say anything. She remembered her birthday party, when everyone had come to swim in her pool —everyone except Rae Jean. Ben had been right.

She held out her hand to Rae Jean. "We're even. The fight's over, OK? No more evil eyes, no more notes, no more voodoo dolls, no nothing. I promise."

"You made a voodoo doll? Of who? Me?"

"Yeah, of you," said Kelly, wishing she hadn't said so much.

"I never knew you hated me that much." Rae Jean's eyes filled with tears.

"I don't," Kelly said quickly. "I never did. You just have a way of making me really mad."

"A voodoo doll?"

"Don't worry. We pulled all the toothpicks back out and threw it away. No more voodoo dolls, I promise."

They shook hands. "No more mud mash. I hated that. I hate worms!"

"Mud *mask,* Rae Jean. Next time, I'll get my mother's expensive mud mask." Kelly laughed. "Can you believe people actually put mud in jars and sell it? We ought to try that sometime. What a way to get rich!"

Rae Jean patted Cinnamon on the head. "I'm so sorry about your parakeet."

Kelly studied Rae Jean closely. She wasn't all that bad, not really. Nobody was *all* bad, or all good for that matter. Even Jennifer argued too much. And Adelaide laughed like a horse. And Ben pestered her all the time. Maybe she hadn't given Rae Jean a chance.

They stood up and walked into the dining room. "Want a popcorn ball?" asked Rae Jean.

"I guess." Kelly picked up a sticky popcorn ball and bit into it.

"You really have a terrible temper, you know that?" Rae Jean said suddenly.

"Me?"

"You've been angry about something or other ever since I moved to this street."

"I have *not*!" shouted Kelly. And then she stopped. She *did* get angry too fast. She had never really thought about it. She wasn't so perfect either. Nobody was.

14
Midnight Is
the Witching Hour

"It was wonderful," whispered Kelly to Jennifer and Adelaide later that night. "He grabbed me just like they do in the movies, and then he kissed me real long and slow."

"Alex?"

"Alex."

"That's enough to make you sick," said Ben.

"Oh, go home, would you, Ben?"

Kelly, Jennifer, Adelaide, and Ben were walking backward down the sidewalk toward the corner of Hopper Street and Bielby Road. They had taken their costumes off and put them back on inside out. "You told us," said Ben, "if you want to see a real live witch, you have to wear your clothes inside out and walk backward to a crossroads at midnight on Halloween."

"That's right."

"Darn. I wish Buster could have come."

"Shhh, be quiet," whispered Kelly.

Midnight is the witching hour.
Then you shall be in my power.

Jennifer repeated the haunting words as she walked slowly backward, feeling her way with her feet. "I'm scared," she said.

"Me, too," said Adelaide. She tripped over a fire hydrant but scrambled quickly back to her feet.

"I do want to see a real witch!" said Kelly. "Now we'll find out once and for all if there are such things as witches."

"Of course there are," said Ben. "I saw a witch last Halloween right outside my window."

"Well, I know we have a ghost living in my attic," said Jennifer. "I'm not kidding. It's the ghost of my great-great-uncle Zachary Jackson. He makes noises up in our attic all the time. He built our house, you know."

"I think I'm going home," said Adelaide, peeking over her shoulder. There was only one more house until they reached the cemetery.

"Chicken," said Jennifer.

"Stop!" They all turned and looked at Kelly. "My ring. It's gone!" she said in a loud whisper.

"Let's see!"

"It's gone! Look." Kelly held out her hand. By the light of the Halloween moon, they all stared at her bare hand. "My powers are gone. I'm completely unprotected!"

Ben studied his new ring, which he had purchased that afternoon from the bubble gum machine at Benchley's Market. "I've got my ring," he said.

"And I've got mine," said Adelaide.

"Without your ring, anything could get you," said Jennifer in her most dramatic voice. She looked up at the sky. "Aliens from other worlds, monsters disguised in human form, ghosts, witches—"

"Stop it!" ordered Kelly. "I'm worried enough."

They turned around and slowly walked past the little church on the corner and into the dark graveyard behind it. When they reached the old Geister mausoleum, they huddled together in a small circle. "That was a special ring," whispered Kelly. "It was a dead man's ring with the full moon ring spell on it. How could I have lost it?"

"Did you take it off somewhere?" asked Jennifer.

"I don't remember taking it off."

"This is a fine time to lose your ring, right here at midnight on Halloween," said Ben.

"Do you think I tried to lose the ring, Ben?"

"You lose everything else," continued Ben. "You lost your lunch money last week, you lost your—"

"Quiet, Ben, or I'll tell Mom you drank all the 7-Up that was hidden in the closet."

"You do and I'll—"

"Shhh!" said Jennifer. She gripped Kelly's arm and pointed to the far corner of the cemetery. Out from the woods floated a ghost! Kelly, Ben, Jennifer, and Adelaide froze as the white specter wove slowly back and forth, gliding from one gravestone to the next. A low moan drifted across the shadowy cemetery. Jennifer's fingers dug deeply into Kelly's arm, but Kelly didn't utter a sound. The ghost floated closer and closer, moaning eerily. Just as they were about to run, the ghost coughed.

"Hey, that's Buster!" said Ben. "I know that cough anywhere!" The ghost fell to the ground, coughing and laughing and twisting about in the tangled sheet. Ben tore the sheet away, and there lay Buster, grinning up at him.

"Scared you, didn't I?"

"Oh, Buster! This is no time for tricks," whispered Kelly.

"I think I'm having a conniption," said Adelaide.

"We're out to see a real witch, a real, live witch at midnight," continued Kelly. "We've got to get quiet."

"Why don't you forget it? There's no such thing as witches," laughed Buster.

Just then a short, high, beeping sound was heard. Ben pressed a button on his watch. "It's midnight, on the dot."

The five witches and warlocks leaned against the cold, granite mausoleum and looked out over the cemetery. "Look!" whispered Adelaide suddenly. She pointed toward the Greeley house, which was dark except for one light in the kitchen. They all sank to the ground and stared as the side door opened with a creaking sound, and out into the moonlight stepped Mrs. Greeley. She held the little black cat in her arms. She laid the cat on the ground, picked up a shovel, and began to dig a hole next to her vegetable garden.

"What's she doing?" whispered Jennifer.

"I don't know," whispered Kelly. "Come on. Let's get closer." They crawled along the ground, through the leaves, around the gravestones, and up to the church.

"She's burying that cat. Look!" said Ben. Mrs. Greeley picked up the lifeless little cat and laid her into the hole.

" 'To gain magical energy and strengthen one's power as a witch, one must bury a good luck charm by the light of the moon,' " chanted Kelly. She looked up at the large moon and back at Mrs. Greeley.

114

"A good luck charm," said Buster, "not a cat."

Adelaide gasped. "A cat *is* a lucky charm, for a witch!"

"Oh, Adelaide," said Kelly.

"It's true!" whispered Adelaide. "Mrs. Greeley is burying a good luck charm by the light of the moon on Halloween at midnight!"

"Let's get out of here," said Jennifer. She stood up. Kelly jumped to her feet and glanced once again across the street. Mrs. Greeley was looking straight at her and motioning her to come across the street.

"Wait!" said Kelly. "She sees us!" She started across the street.

"Where are you going?" whispered Jennifer, pulling at Kelly's inside-out sleeve.

"Come on," ordered Kelly. The five of them walked slowly across the street and stood facing Mrs. Greeley.

"What are you doing with the shovel, Mrs. Greeley?" asked Kelly.

"Goodness gracious, aren't you children out rather late tonight?" asked Rae Jean's mother. Nobody said a word, so she continued. "I had to bury that poor little cat that came to our door tonight. She died a few minutes ago. It's all for the best. She was so very sick." She smiled, but only her mouth seemed to smile. Her eyes never smiled.

" 'Midnight is the witching hour,' " mumbled Adelaide. "*You* wrote that note!"

"Adelaide!" said Kelly. She backed up.

"What note?" asked Mrs. Greeley, taking a step forward.

"Nothing!" said Kelly. "We really must go."

"Oh, wait! I have so many cookies left over from the party. Let me get you some. Come on inside." Mrs. Greeley held out her hand to Kelly. Kelly looked at her hand. A gold ring with a red stone glittered on her finger.

"That's my ring!" said Kelly. "Where'd you find it?"

"Oh, this?" Mrs. Greeley pulled the ring from her finger and held it out. "I wondered whose ring this was. I found it on the counter by the sink. Here."

Kelly reached for the gold ring and slid it back on her finger. "Thanks!" She turned and ran down the sidewalk.

"No, wait!" cried Mrs. Greeley.

"We've got to get home," said Kelly. The children ran as fast as they could all the way down Hopper Street. Kelly's heart was pounding as she opened the front door, pulled Ben inside, and quietly closed it behind them. They tiptoed into the kitchen and sat down at the table. The moon cast its eerie, yellow light across the room.

"She's a real live witch!" whispered Kelly.

"Who?"

"Mrs. Greeley! Didn't you see her?"

"Sure I did. She was burying a dead cat. So what? If I had a sick cat that died, I'd bury it, too."

"But Ben, she was burying it at midnight on Halloween!"

"The cat died at midnight on Halloween. When else could she bury it?"

"She could have waited until tomorrow. She must be a witch!"

"There's no such thing as witches. That's ridiculous."

"Who says? She took my ring, didn't she? I don't remember putting my ring on the counter," whispered Kelly. She twisted the ring around and around on her finger.

"You *must* have. You're always losing things."

"I am not!"

"You are, too."

"She's a witch," stated Kelly. "She even sent us a spooky note on her very own witch stationery. I saw it. Some of that blue stationery was right on her kitchen counter."

"Rae Jean could have tacked that note to the tree."

"You think so?"

"I don't know." Ben slid off his chair and tiptoed into the family room. Kelly followed him into the darkened room. Ben crawled behind the sofa and pulled out a large plastic pumpkin filled with candy. He grabbed a candy bar, ripped off the wrapper, and bit into it.

"Lemme have a piece," said Kelly. Ben dumped the candy from the pumpkin onto the floor and began to count all the candy bars.

"You should have gone trick or treating," he said with his mouth full of chocolate and peanuts and caramel. "Mmmm, this is good. A tasty little midnight snack."

"Please, Ben?"

"You should have gotten some of Mrs. Greeley's cookies. She was going to give us some."

"Huh uh! I was too scared!" Ben popped a candy kiss into his mouth. "Come on, Ben. Give me some!"

"Here. You can have this licorice."

"Thanks!" Kelly took the licorice and bit off the end of it. Suddenly she thought about the box of candles in Mrs. Greeley's attic. She remembered how she had reached for one and how Mrs. Greeley had stopped her. Maybe those *were* special candles. Special witch candles. Why would anyone have that many purple candles? And why wouldn't Mrs. Greeley let her touch them?

"Mrs. Greeley *is* a witch," said Kelly. "She is, Ben, I'm sure of it."

"You know what?" said Ben. He stared out the window at the large orange moon and the black trees, and then looked straight at Kelly. "She just might be!"

"You think so?"

"Who knows? Anything's possible on Halloween."

About the Author

LINDA GONDOSCH received her Master's in English from North Kentucky University. She was inspired to write this book after her daughter, Lisa, posing as Madame Venezuela, set up a fortune-teller's stand—complete with crystal ball—at an eighth-grade carnival. She is the author of *Who Needs a Bratty Brother?*, and *Who's Afraid of Haggerty House?*, published by Minstrel Books, which are also about Kelly McCoy. Ms. Gondosch lives in Lawrenceburg, Indiana, with her family.

About the Illustrator

HELEN COGANCHERRY attended the Philadelphia College of Art and has illustrated many books, including the "Kelly McCoy" stories. She loves museums and finds that wherever she goes she thinks of possible pictures. She has three children and lives in Wallingford, Pennsylvania.